Praise for
The Guest Book Trilogy

The Man in Cabin Number Five
Book One

"Masterfully written. An entertaining work that will keep the reader hooked until the end. Congratulations on an exceptional book." *Readers' Favorite*

"An engaging drama with a strong cast and a final surprise." *Kirkus Review*

The Girls in Cabin Number Three
Book Two

"This book takes up where *The Man in Cabin Number Five* left off, with plenty of intrigue in the idyllic mountain locale." *Susan Denley, former Associate Features Editor, Los Angeles Times*

"With themes of love, family, friendship, new beginnings, and the complexity of life, readers will get hooked from the very beginning." *San Francisco Book Review*

The Starlet in Cabin Number Seven
Book Three

"*The Starlet in Cabin Number Seven* feels like catching up with old friends as the narrative amiably revisits the highlights of Lake Arrowhead... A light and engaging read, with an enticing mountain setting." *Kirkus Review*

"Braun's storytelling skill and pacing are engaging and evocative, making this book a delightful read for fans of cozy mysteries and those who appreciate stories of hope, redemption, and the enduring bonds of friendship. Reading The Starlet was a heartwarming experience, like revisiting a beloved place and old friends." *Readers' Favorite*

Dear Noah: The Conclusion
Book Five

"Having lived in Lake Arrowhead for many years, Chrysteen Braun's books continually remind me of just how wonderful it is to live up here. It's been fun figuring out places both real and fictional. Her storytelling skillfully blends relationships, rich characters and unexpected endings, all set in our delightful mountain towns." *Angela Yap, Editor, Mountain News, Lake Arrowhead, CA*

When the Daffodils Bloom: Charlotte's Story
Book Six

"Braun masterfully balances heartache with healing, creating a story that lingers long after the final page. It's a celebration of second chances—in life, in love, and in the pursuit of long-forgotten dreams." *Kate Osborn, formerly with the Mountain News, Lake Arrowhead, CA*

THE MAIDSERVANT IN CABIN NUMBER ONE

THE BEGINNING

CHRYSTEEN BRAUN

Also by Chrysteen Braun

The Guest Book Trilogy
The Man in Cabin Number Five, Book One
The Girls in Cabin Number Three, Book Two
The Starlet in Cabin Number Seven, Book Three
The Maidservant in Cabin Number One, The Beginning, Book Four
Dear Noah, The Conclusion, Book Five
When the Daffodils Bloom, Book Six

Coming Soon
Family Portrait

Design and distribution by Bublish, Inc.

ISBN: 978-1-647048-08-2 (eBook)
ISBN: 978-1-647048-07-5 (paperback)
ISBN: 978-1-647048-09-9 (hardcover)

To my husband, Larry.
Always the wind beneath my wings.

Part One

Ruth Ann Landry

CHAPTER ONE

My father died when I was young, leaving me and my mother alone in a one-bedroom apartment, that even with my mother's meager wages, they'd barely afforded. Mostly, her earnings helped pay for our heat, and now, with my father gone, we were often so cold, we sometimes wore three or four layers of clothing. Weather in Seattle was always unpredictable; even during the dead of winter, it could be foggy and raining in the mornings and clear and sunny in the afternoons. I remember the skies were mostly gray.

But maybe that was because of how we lived.

We originally came from rural Nashville, Tennessee, way before it became famous for country music. I was five, and I don't recall much about our home there; but what I do remember was that my father was a drinker. When he was sober, he was my idol. He'd read to me at bedtime, and then when it was time for me to go to sleep, he'd tuck me in so snugly, he'd say "you're snug as a bug." He was always coming up behind my mother while she was at the sink, giving her a hug, snuggling her neck, or grabbing her caboose, as he called it.

During the day, he worked for the railway, and at the end of his long shift, he spent his nights drinking at the local bar. He called it is "winding down place."

My mother worked at the gunpowder plant.

After the 1918 train wreck, they laid my father off while the tracks could be repaired, and he took this as a premonition he would permanently lose his job. For months he hung around the house until one day, my mother pointed out that we needed his wages to survive and she suggested he look for a job at the powder plant where she worked.

When she said this, I could see the wheels moving around in his head; he silently worked his mouth, chewing his cheek. Then he pushed his tongue around his teeth, pushing his upper lip out.

"I ain't gonna work at some woman's job," he said, an edge rising in his voice...

That was the first time I remember him hauling off and hitting her.

Eventually, they called him back to the railway, but by this time he'd been drinking so much, even I could smell the alcohol coming through his pores. The first day he went back, they fired him.

My mother never said a word, but my father took that as a silent accusation of his failure, and he raised his arm to strike her. That was the second time he hit her. Over the next few weeks, it got worse. One day, thinking I could stop him, I gallantly stood in front of my mother and acted as her shield.

"Get outta my way," he yelled.

He pushed his mouth forward and pursed his lips before he backhanded me and knocked me down. I fell flat on my back and I instantly felt the wind leave my lungs. I couldn't breathe and I thought for sure I was going to die. When my mother kneeled beside me, he kicked her, and when she tried to get up, he kicked her again.

After that, he was gone for two days, and when he returned, I stood in our doorway and said, "If you touch me or my mother again, I swear I'll kill you in your sleep."

"Shut up," he said, pushing me down. "We're going to where I can find a better job."

In 1919, we made it west to Seattle, and to my father's credit, he found a job at the Spokane, Portland & Seattle Railway. By the end of that year, my mother answered an ad for a maid's position for a wealthy financier who owned a hilltop mansion in the Harvard-Belmont Historic Landmark District.

While I had no actual plan to actually kill my father, for a while, I thought he took my death threat seriously. He still drank, but he left us alone, and we made it a point to stay out of his way if he was riled. My mother sometimes worked until all hours of the evening, so I learned to make our meals. The first few times my father didn't come home for dinner, I thought maybe he too had to stay late, so I'd cover his dinner and set it on the table. But then his drinking got worse, and even if I was sound asleep, his body odor and sour breath would wake me. Prohibition had no impact on him finding something to drink. After about a week of this, I quit making his dinner. This infuriated him, but I was wasting the little money we had on food that had to be dumped into the garbage because he didn't eat it.

That Christmas of 1920, like so many in the past, we had no tree, and there were no packages to open. My mother brought home some leftovers Cook had prepared for the servants, and she and I sat and ate them. When my father finally came home, he'd been drinking, and wanted to know where his dinner was.

"There was just enough for me and Ruthie," my mother said calmly.

"Well, then, you won't get to eat either," he said, reaching for her plate and throwing it, food and all, on to the floor. Instinctively, my mother jumped from her chair and pulled me to her. I know she was thinking she'd be able to protect me from his rage. As he'd done before, he shoved me to the side and grabbed my mother's arm, twisting it until she cried out in pain.

He finally released her, but not before he threw my plate on the floor, too. Then he stomped out of the apartment and didn't come home until the next evening.

On New Year's Eve, my mother worked late to help with the party at the mansion. I made myself a simple dinner of bread and cheese, and then I went to play Parcheesi with the girl who lived next door. At midnight, we watched the fireworks from her apartment window, and then I came back home. I lit the kerosene lamp that sat on the kitchen table and fully intended to read *The Swiss Family Robinson* book she'd lent me, but I fell asleep.

It was still dark out when the door to our apartment burst open, crashing against the wall and jolting me awake. Even in the dim light of the streetlamp outside our window, I could tell it was my father. I even smelled him. I jumped to my feet and there in the threshold he stood, drunker than a skunk. His eyes squinted as he tried to determine who it was that had been sitting at our table, and then when he figured out it was me, he looked around for my mother, who hadn't returned from work yet.

"Where the hell is she?" he bellowed.

I didn't give him the satisfaction of an answer, which made him furious. He staggered to the table and picked up my book and began ripping pages from it.

"*Stop!*" I yelled.

But he kept on tearing pages and watching them fall to the floor. He came around the right-hand side of the table as I backed closer to the sink. I hoped to give myself space enough to run from the apartment, but even though he tripped on the leg of the table, he was quicker than I was. He grabbed my left arm as I grabbed onto the sink. I kicked him in the shin and he momentarily released me, giving me just enough time to turn and pick up our cast iron pan.

When he looked up at me, I swung the pan at him with all my might. He fell to the floor, out cold. Suddenly, my mother was there, standing in the doorway, and she looked in horror, first at me, and then at my father.

"Dear god," she said, dropping her bag on the table. "Help me get him up. He's bleeding."

I'd broken his nose, and his face was black and blue for two weeks.

My name is Ruth Ann Landry, but most people called me Ruthie.

CHAPTER TWO

One Sunday evening in 1922, a man from the railroad came to tell us my father was killed when a rail yard worker accidentally released eighty feet of coal onto him and another man. He hemmed and hawed while he stood at the door, and I could tell he was uncomfortable by the way he shifted from foot to foot. Even though it was a cool evening, he wiped sweat from his forehead with his shirtsleeve and I saw a drop escape his sideburns and run down his face. My mother instinctively reached for me, as though I could console her. Even though I'd mentally detached myself from my father, I went to her when she held her arms out to me. I couldn't understand how she could still care about him, but she cried, and said, "Now what are we going to do?"

I didn't truly understand what she meant until I realized we'd now have less money for food and rent.

As if answering her question, the man said, "There's a twenty-five dollar death policy that'll be comin' soon."

Eventually 1922 rolled into 1923, and my mother was still one of the many servants at the mansion. There was the head housekeeper, who reported directly to the mistress and ran the household, the senior housemaid, who reported to the head housekeeper, and the housemaid, (or maidservant), who was an "in between" maid. My mother's position was that of the parlor maid, and she was responsible for keeping the reception and living rooms tidy, answering the door, announcing the arrival of guests, serving refreshments and then dinner.

There were two cooks who prepared all the food for the household, and a scullery maid who scrubbed the stoves, pots and pans and kitchen floors.

A live-in nanny took care of their three children.

I was ten then, when my mother told me the maidservant, or the "in between" maid, was let go. It wasn't that she hadn't performed her duties well, she said confidentially; it was that she became unfit for employment. Seeing an opportunity for me to help support our household, my mother mentioned me for the position and she told me to prepare for my interview. She rummaged through our clothes cupboard and pulled a dress from a hanger.

"This is the best I can do," she said, making me try it on. "Stop squirming."

"Ow," I cried out.

She'd pinned the back of the dress to make it tighter, and when I moved, one of the pins pricked my skin.

Two days later, I stood in front of the head housekeeper in my new uniform; a shorter white dress with balloon sleeves, a white apron with an eyelet trimmed bodice, white stocking and shoes, but no head covering. Although there was no wedding ring, she was called Mrs. Goodspeed. (With a name like that, I would have thought she was from England, but she had no accent.) She was older than God, although I did not know how old that would be. Her gray hair was tightly combed back and tied in a bun, and her eyes bored into me like they could set me on fire. She wore a black long-sleeved dress with a black and white geometric print yoke, which was repeated on her sleeves. On her belt hung a chain of keys, no doubt for every room in the house. She wore black shoes and stockings.

My mother's uniform was also a black long-sleeved dress, but with a starched white long apron with eyelet accents on the bodice, a white ruffled cap, and those same black shoes and stockings. Each servant wore the basic black, but to differentiate them, their apron bodices were different.

My mother had warned me about fidgeting, and it took everything I had in me to stand there and listen to Mrs. Goodspeed while she recited the household rules.

"You will arrive at six each morning to dress into your costume and you will wait for the family to rise. When you leave, you must fold and place your garments in the laundry. You will stand still and look at the person when you're being spoken to and keep your hands folded in front of you. Never speak to the master or mistress unless it's delivering a message, and never offer an opinion, say good morning or good night. No smoking, gambling, or foul language. We will deduct any damages or breakage from your wages. No visitors, whether they're a friend or relative, are to be introduced into the servant's hall without the consent of the head housekeeper."

She took a breath, and I let mine out.

"No followers are allowed, and any maid found fraternizing with a member of the opposite sex will be dismissed. If you don't understand what that means, ask your mother. And finally, no one is to be admitted into the house without the consent of the parlor maid or the head cook. And then, it must be between the hours of nine and three. You will clean the bedrooms and bathing chambers, and once that has been done, you'll make sure the laundry has been cleaned and replenished, fill the lamps, and beat the rugs. Any questions?"

She didn't wait for me to answer.

"Good."

Thankfully, I wouldn't be required to take up residence in the house, although living in such a grand place would be *something*. It was hard for me to imagine *anyone* having such a beautiful place to live. I was grateful my hours would be the same as my mother's, so I wouldn't have to make my own way in the dark hours of the morning or evening.

Since the family wasn't up yet, my first stop was the kitchen. When Cook set aside a plate with a biscuit and jam for me, I knew I had at least one other ally in the house besides my mother. I was starving, and when I finished, Cook watched as I licked my fingers to pick up the crumbs on the plate.

"You can only have one, now," she said. "Mrs. Goodspeed makes us account for all the food we prepare."

"Will someone show me what I'm supposed to do?" I asked my mother.

"I'll ask if I can accompany you if I'm not busy with my work," she said.

By seven, the nanny had the children up and dressed, so I started in the daughters' rooms first. Large pink and green bouquets of flowers covered their walls, and the bedspread and curtains were the same pattern, but with pink trim. There was so much going on, at first it made me dizzy. I'd never seen anything like it, so I took it all in before I got started. I gathered the nightdresses and the clothing that needed laundering and took them downstairs. Next, I cleaned their bathing rooms and then realized I hadn't taken their soiled towels down with the other washing. After making a second trip downstairs, I quickly learned that if I gathered up *all* the laundry, I could avoid unnecessary trips up and down the stairs.

The boy's bedroom wallpaper had colorful squirrels, rabbits, ponies and treehouses on it, and the bedding and draperies were in the same colors but in a plaid pattern. I'd never seen anything like it. Clothes were strewn about the floor, and when I bent to pick them up, I noticed there were spots on the wallpaper where the boy must have been picking at it. I wondered if he'd gotten into trouble for doing that. Or was he spoiled?

Once the master and mistress were up, I cleaned their rooms and brought in new towels. They had printed paper on their walls also, but it was much more subdued. I pulled the draperies back to let in daylight and checked the rugs to see if they needed cleaning. I wasn't sure if I needed to beat them every day; I would have to ask Mrs. Goodspeed when I saw her.

When I finished my chores, I realized I had time to spare, but I wasn't sure what I should do. I went back down to the kitchen, where Cook had set out some bread and meat, and she made me a sandwich.

"Now don't go thinkin' I'm going to make you all your meals," she said, winking at me.

"No ma'am," I answered. "I've finished, and was wondering if I should ask Mrs. Goodspeed what I should do next?"

Cook wrinkled her forehead and said, "I think you'll be asking for trouble if you ask for more work, but it's up to you."

"Well, I can't just sit here. I'll really get into trouble then."

She sighed. "Okay then. You sit here. You can't be roaming around the house. I'll go find her."

A few minutes later, both women returned.

"What's this then?" Mrs. Goodspeed asked, raising her eyebrow.

I jumped out of my chair and stood before her, remembering to keep my hands still.

"I've finished for the morning, ma'am, and I wondered if you had something else for me to do?"

"Well, let's see about that," she said, and turned to leave. "Follow me, then."

Her impatience with me was clear in her brisk steps, and I had a hard time keeping up with her. When we got to the first room, she knocked, and then opened the door.

"Hmph," she said as she went inside.

She checked the bedding, and the bathing room, and when she seemed to be satisfied, she turned to me and raised an eyebrow. She opened the other two bedroom doors and did the same.

"Hmph."

Her cool eyes narrowed slightly, reminding me of a cat I once saw getting ready to pounce on its victim.

"Well, we'll certainly find you something else to do. Follow me."

We made our way down the back hall and into the kitchen.

"It seems our little imp here has idle hands, and that just won't do," she said to Cook. "Certainly, you can find something for her to do here in the kitchen. Give her another apron so she doesn't soil her costume."

"And you," she said, turning to me, "will find something to do down here until you help set the table, serve dinner and remove the dishes. After which you will turn down the bedding for the children and the master and mistress. Cook will find something for you to do." She looked at me from the corner of her eye and left.

"Here," Cook said, "you can peel these potatoes. My back is killing me."

I peeled potatoes and carrots, and filled the cooking pot with water, before I realized it was too heavy to set it on the stove to boil. Cook watched me as I struggled, then came to my rescue.

"And what have you just learned?" she asked.

"To put a little water in the pot, and then use two or three smaller containers to fill it up."

Cook had me take the bread out of the oven and set it on racks to cool, and then I rolled flour dough for pies and pastries. I learned to take the delivery of butter, sugar, eggs, fruit, and flour and then put it all away once Cook checked the order. I took the folded laundry upstairs to the bedrooms and returned to the kitchen. After dinner, I realized I could have saved myself a trip had I brought the laundry up when I went up to turn the beds down.

After walking home with my mother, I barely took the time to change into my bedclothes before I fell into my bed. I was exhausted. My mother massaged my feet and within minutes, I was asleep.

CHAPTER THREE

The first few days, I'd only had glimpses of the children who lived in the house. Nellie was a year older than I was; she was eleven. Abigail was nine, and Francis was seven. Sometimes when I was cleaning their rooms, the three of them peeked in to watch me. The minute I saw them, I froze, and I was sure my eyes were as wide as saucers. I looked at the three of them, and then they giggled and ran back into the hallway.

Once, while I was cleaning Nellie's room, she crept in and closed the door behind her. She stood motionless as I went about my work. I almost jumped out of my skin when I realized she was there, but I pretended I hadn't seen her, and kept dusting her furniture.

"You're my age," she finally said.

"I think I am. I'm ten."

"I'm eleven. This is the first time we've had a girl."

"What do you mean by that?" I asked.

"I only meant our other maids were older. Did you know the last one got pregnant?"

I stopped dead in my tracks and turned to look at her.

"Do you know what that means?" she asked.

"Of course I do, silly."

Then I realized the mistake I'd made addressing her that way.

"I'm so sorry. I didn't mean to call you silly."

"It's okay. My sister calls me that all the time. I think it's because she doesn't understand what I'm talking about sometimes. I'm Nellie. That's short for Cornelia. When she was young, Abigail couldn't pronounce my name and kept calling me that, so it stuck."

"I'm Ruth Ann, but everyone calls me Ruthie. I think your name is much prettier than mine."

"I don't know," Nellie said thoughtfully. "I kind of like Ruthie."

Footsteps outside her door silenced both of us.

"Hurry," I whispered. "Get under the bed."

Suddenly, there was a knock on the door, and Mrs. Goodspeed stood there with her arms folded over her chest. Her eyes narrowed—which I'd quickly learned was a means to disarm her inferiors—and she quickly scanned the room.

"Who were you talking to?"

"No one, ma'am," I said, continuing with my work.

"I could have sworn I heard you talking to someone."

"I'm afraid I've begun talking to myself, ma'am. It helps me remember all that I have to do."

"Hmph," she said as she stepped into the room. She craned her neck to look beyond the beds, and when she didn't see anything, she grumbled again. "Hmph."

And with that, she turned and left.

Nellie waited a few minutes before she came out from under the bed, and then we both burst out in giggles.

"Shh," I whispered.

"Mrs. Goodspeed is such a grump," she said, plopping down onto her freshly made bed.

"Be careful," I said. "I just made that bed up. And why do you both sometimes sleep in this tiny bed?"

She laid back and put her folded arms beneath her head. Ignoring me, she sighed.

"Because Abigail likes me to read to her, and she prefers my bed. What's it like being a maid?" she asked.

13

Before I could think, I blurted out, "Well, it's not much fun. My feet are always tired, and I work six days a week. My pay isn't much, and I have to turn all my money over to my mother. We barely get by, you know."

Nellie's brows rose in surprise.

"Plus, I'm always hungry."

"Oh," she said, tilting her head in thought. She quickly changed the subject. "Well, I'm sure the coast is clear by now. I should go find Nanny."

When she got up, I don't know why I was surprised she didn't straighten out her bed.

"Ta ta," she said before she stuck her head out the door to make sure the coast was clear.

A few weeks before Christmas, Cook enlisted help from anyone with spare time to help string cranberry garland for the tree. I must have threaded and tied twenty sections of berries together, and it all sat at my feet when my mother came in to check on me.

"She does such a good job, we'll have to call her the cranberry queen," Cook said, chuckling. "This year, the Mistress wants to add dried orange slices, so when you're done there, I could use your help getting them cut up and put on cookie sheets. You know, there's no rest for the weary."

I thought we'd never finish, but we did and a few days later, voices from downstairs caught my attention. From the top of the stairs, I stood in wonder as several men brought in the most wonderful evergreen tree for the grand entry hall. Once they figured out how to keep it from leaning, they brought in a ladder and one climbed it while the other handed up the tinsel and the orange and berry garlands.

Mrs. Goodspeed joined them soon and, with a long stick, pointed to where she wanted the candles and mercury ball ornaments hung. Once they got down to the lower level, the children were allowed to hang their handmade paper ornaments. Even with the bottom of the tree so higgledy-piggledy, I'd never seen such an amazing sight.

Each day, I noticed more gifts had been added beneath the tree, and while I knew in my heart there would be nothing for me or my mother, I hoped beyond hope. On Christmas Eve day, I helped Cook prepare a delicious meal of maple-bourbon turkey, crusted roast beef, bread stuffing, Brussels sprouts with pecans and bacon, roasted potatoes, salmon, and apple pie.

After dinner, while we cleared the table, the family gathered around the tree, now with all the candles lit, and sang Christmas carols. Hearing a commotion in the living room, I rushed in from a side doorway just as the children raced in to find Santa brushing himself off, like he'd just come down the chimney. He handed out even more gifts from his huge red bag, and then winked at me before he slid from the room.

Back in the kitchen, the servants all gathered around our table and we ate most of what was left of dinner.

"Just be thankful we have such a wonderful meal to eat," my mother said, as if reading my mind. "Next year, we'll have our own gifts."

After we cleared our table and put the leftovers away, Cook came to me with a small wrapped gift.

"Santa left this for you," she said, handing it to me.

I knew that wasn't true, for I didn't really believe in Santa—but I couldn't believe my luck.

"Look, Mother," I said, beaming.

"I see it. Open it."

Never having seen such fancy wrapping, I carefully undid the package, and quickly saw there were two books. One was *The Swiss Family Robinson*, and the other was *The Wonderful Wizard of Oz*.

I thought for sure I was the luckiest girl alive.

One spring day while I was cleaning Nellie's bedroom, she burst through the door and cried, "Ruthie. Ruthie. Come to the window and look!"

I instinctively turned to check that Mrs. Goodspeed hadn't followed behind her before I made my way to the window. There, in their yard, stood a man with a black pony. Francis was dressed in western gear and sitting in the saddle, holding the pony's reins in his small hands.

"I'm too old for that, of course, but I always love it when the pony comes to visit. Did you ever have your picture taken on a pony?"

She looked so innocent right then. I couldn't be angry with her for being so dumb. Of course, I'd never had my picture taken with a pony. No one in their right mind would come in to our neighborhood, where it was so obvious no one could afford such a luxury as a photo.

"Oh my," Nellie said, covering her mouth with her hand. "The pony has just pooped and I'm sure when the head gardener sees it, he'll have a fit. He'll send the boy out to clean it up before Father comes home."

"That poor horse looks tired," I said.

"Well, he's almost done, and then he can go home."

"I doubt it. I'm sure he'll have to go around the entire neighborhood first, poor thing."

"*He's just a pony,*" Nellie said. "*It's his job.*"

I looked at her like she was the dumbest person I knew.

"*What?*" she asked.

She glanced in her dressing-table mirror and straightened out a barrette.

That afternoon when I saw Cook, I tried to explain to her what Nellie said, and how frustrated I was with her for being so dense. Of course, I didn't use that word in case someone overheard our conversation. She nodded to me as she kept working, occasionally glancing at me. Finally, she stopped cutting potatoes and set her knife down. She went into the pantry and came out with something wrapped in cloth.

"Grab a couple pieces of bread," she said, cutting two slices of cheddar cheese. "Food will fix just about anything," she said, putting the cheese on the bread and wrapping it all up.

CHAPTER FOUR

In the fall, they replaced the nanny with a governess and they officially made the nursery into a lessons room where the children were schooled. In a few years, Francis would be sent to private school, but Nellie and Abigail would continue to be taught from home. I wasn't sure what prompted Mrs. Goodspeed to add yet another chore to my already full day, but I ended up being responsible for keeping the room neat and orderly.

Whatever the children learned, they were not being taught to pick up after themselves. At the end of each day, I picked up loose papers that had been strewn across the floor and I sorted through pencils and crayons and put them in their proper holders. If they didn't mark their books with their place, I put them back in the bookcases that lined one wall. It was a good thing I knew how to read, for every book was shelved alphabetically.

One afternoon, I sorted through some papers that Francis and Abigail had left out. I'd never had my own set of crayons, so I sat at the long desk and began to color in some images they'd drawn. My heart raced as I listened for sounds that someone could be approaching, which just added to the excitement of it all. I was so nervous, I accidentally broke the red crayon in half. If they found me out, I'd certainly be let go, so I figured I had two choices. One was to put the Crayola back in the box and let the children discover it and blame each other, or my other option was to take it with me and throw it away with the trash.

I decided the color would certainly be missed, so I put it back in its box and tucked my artwork into the middle of the stack of papers before I left the room.

A piano teacher came to the house every week and gave all three children their music lessons. Down in the kitchen, Cook and I would chuckle when it was Francis' turn to play. To put it bluntly, he was not the least bit musically inclined. Even when he practiced, which the governess made him do every day, the sound of missed notes filled the entire bottom floor. Nellie was better, but Abigail definitely had an ear for music. I tried to pace my time in the kitchen to be there when she played.

A master chess player came in to teach Francis to play chess, and a sailing instructor came, no matter the weather, to teach him how to sail. Nellie and Abigail had regular dance lessons taught by a young woman who came to the house three times a week. I wasn't at all interested in chess, but on the days the girls danced, I'd find myself swaying to the music as I stood in the doorway to the lessons room. If Nellie saw me there, she'd wave, but Abigail would stomp her foot to remind her they weren't to fraternize with the likes of me.

The year Nellie turned twelve, she started her period. I saw the blood on her bed sheet and pointed it out to the laundress, who in turn, asked Cook what she should do.

"*About what?*" Cook asked. "Get the necessaries and go fetch the doctor. He can explain it all to Miss Nellie, but in the meantime, you can show her what to do. And soak that sheet in cold water."

Even with my wages, we were still behind in our rent and with no relief in sight, our landlord gave us two options. We could either move into a one-room apartment in the same building and pay off our debt in monthly installments, or we would be put out on the street. My mother chose the first option. The move would take effect immediately, so we had no time to go through our belongings before we dragged everything up two sets of dark, narrow stairs to our fifteen by fifteen foot room.

It smelled musty, like it had been closed up for a while. At one time, someone had painted the walls a green color, but wash marks over the years wiped away most of the color in some spots. It was obvious where pictures used to be hung for just the opposite had happened; the walls were darker. The floor was a dark unfinished wood, and there was one spot where it loudly creaked where we walked. I hoped there wasn't a tenant below us, for if there was, they'd be pounding on their ceiling for us to be quiet. The room had a bed, a dresser, a small table with two chairs, a sink for washing dishes, a wood stove, and shelves for storing kitchen items.

We dumped everything on the floor, and that first night, we dug through the piles of clothing and linens to find our bedding; we left everything else in a jumble. We shoved the boxes of knickknacks along one wall so we wouldn't kill ourselves if we had to get up in the middle of the night to go down the hall to the toilet. The only things we put away were our few dishes, pots, pans, and silverware, so we could have something to eat with the next morning.

My mother and I only had Sunday afternoons off, so until then, we sorted through a few things to wear until we could get to the mansion and change into our uniforms.

When I turned thirteen, I started my "monthlies" as my mother called them. I'd already talked the laundress into giving me a used belt and some pads, so I was prepared. I'd begun to wonder if I would ever have my time, and more than once, Nellie asked me if I'd "started" yet. She wasn't the slightest bit embarrassed to talk about it, but I was. In fact, the first time I bled on my sheet, I thought I was going to die of embarrassment when my mother found the blood, and set the sheet in cold water to get the stain out.

"It's a good thing we have two sheets," she said.

That morning, when I went into the kitchen to help Cook, she said, "Well, our little girl is growing up."

I just rolled my eyes, but inwardly I was fit to be tied.

CHAPTER FIVE

For three years, I'd attended to the master and mistress of the mansion, Franklin and Rose Mary Fletcher, but I'd never had the occasion of dealing with either of them other than serving or clearing the table. I sometimes felt Mr. Fletcher's eyes following me as I performed my duties, and it made me so nervous, one time I spilled coffee on his saucer as I poured it.

He touched my arm, as if to warn me, and while the touch itself wasn't harsh, it was hot, and for some reason it reminded me of the times when my father was drunk and grabbed me or my mother. I never looked Mr. Fletcher in the eye, for fear he'd recognize the alarm I felt. After that, I was extra careful to make sure I served with perfection, for I didn't want any unwelcomed attention.

That night, I asked my mother if she ever thought about my father.

"He was not always like that," she said.

I never pursued the subject.

It was sometime later that I put too much gravy on Mr. Fletcher's mashed potatoes, and I felt two fingers on my arm. They almost scalded my skin. I kept my head bowed, but I was certain I'd seen Mrs. Fletcher look in my direction.

When I was fourteen, they offered my mother and me two empty rooms in the servant's quarters upstairs. Her first thought was that we'd be guaranteed a roof over our heads, and mine was that the rooms would most likely be small and this would bring me closer to the master and mistress; I wasn't sure how I felt about that.

Once again, we sorted through our belongings, gathering what we wouldn't need so we could sell it all to the peddler who regularly drove his cart on our street. By then, I had four books, and I carefully wrapped them in one of our blankets. We gathered our possessions and put everything into two pillowcases.

The rooms upstairs were small, but each had a single bed, a dresser, and a nightstand with an oil lamp. I'd seen an old crate in the pantry and asked Cook if I could have it.

"Of course," she said.

As I was bringing it up the back stairs, I ran into Mr. Fletcher, who was coming down. As was the custom, I stepped aside and lowered my eyes to let him pass, but instead of continuing on, he stopped.

"And what do you have there?" he asked, not unkindly.

My first instinct was to tell him only that I found it, but then I was afraid he would think I stole it.

"I found it for my books, and Cook said she didn't need it. I hope that's not a problem, sir," I said.

He thought about it for a minute, then replied, "I think it's a perfect shelf for your books. Do you like to read?"

"Yes, sir. I do."

"Well, let's see if we can find you something you haven't read yet. I'm sure Nellie has some books you could have."

Suddenly, any trepidation I had about him dissolved. A man who liked books couldn't be all that horrible.

"Thank you, sir," I said.

"So I understand you now have your own room," he said.

"Yes, sir. It's very exciting."

"Well, I'll let you get to it then." And with that, he was off down the stairs.

I never thought to question what he was doing upstairs.

For my fifteenth birthday, Cook baked me a cake. After we'd served dinner to the household and cleared the table, the servants gathered in the kitchen, and we had our dinner.

"I baked your favorite," Cook said. "I couldn't spare a new candle, so it looks like you'll never grow old." She lit the used candle and then brought the cake to the table where most of the staff gathered.

So that we wouldn't be reprimanded for singing, everyone whispered, "Happy Birthday, Ruthie."

I made a quick wish and then blew out the candle before it burned down too far to be able to be used again.

I unwrapped Mother's gift; it was another book to add to my collection, *Pollyanna*. Cook gave me a journal, some pencils and a sharpener.

"To write your thoughts down," she said.

"If the weather holds up, on Sunday afternoon, we can walk to the bookshop and then have a soda at the drugstore," my mother said.

How could I refuse? Those were two of my favorite things to do.

On Sunday a cool wind was blowing in from the north, but it was tolerable if we wore our sweaters. One of the best things about living in the house was that both Mother and I had extra money to set aside each month. I counted out two dollars and tucked it into my sweater pocket. As we walked, I periodically checked to make sure it was still there, and that I hadn't lost it somewhere along the way.

The bookshop opened one Sunday a month, and I could barely contain myself when I opened the door and heard a bell signal our entry. We spent over an hour going through all the aisles of books, and when the shop owner came to tell us the store was closing, I finally made my decision. I bought Agatha Christie's first book, *The Mysterious Affair at Styles*.

It was getting late, but I still wanted a soda, so we rushed to the drugstore and found two stools at the counter.

"This has been the best day ever," I told my mother.

We were back at the mansion before it got dark, which was the rule. We came in through the back door, and I proudly showed Cook my purchase.

"I'll be up all night reading," I told her.

That next week, I was in the kitchen when Cook answered the back door to a young man delivering her weekly grocery order. I went to the window above the sink and looked out at his delivery truck, and instead of old Mr. Gregory, a handsome younger man was unloading bags of flour and sugar.

I stepped back into the hallway so I could peer around the doorway to watch as he brought everything in and put it all in the pantry. Although it was gray outside, it was warm, and he grew warm from the work and wiped his brow with his arm.

"Thank you, Andrew," Cook said, giving him a few coins as a tip. "And here's next week's order."

"Welcome, ma'am," he said, tilting his cap to her.

"Who was that?" I asked once he was gone.

"Never you mind, little lady," she said, raising her eyebrow. She meant to look at me sternly, but she was nowhere near as threatening as Mrs. Goodspeed. "Young boys are trouble. And you don't need any trouble."

"Well, I can look, can't I?"

"You have plenty of time, dear one. We don't want you goin' and gettin' in trouble now, if you get my drift."

"Hmph," I said.

The rules were no followers, but I couldn't help wondering how a young woman could go about meeting someone when she was cooped up in the house every day.

As if she read my mind, when I went to Nellie's room to bring her clean laundry, she asked, "Did you see our new delivery boy?"

"In passing, I did."

"Well, I think he's quite handsome, but of course he's beneath my station. That is, unless I married him when he became my grocer." She thought for a moment, and then said, "I don't think that would work either. Oh, well."

With that, she turned and left her room.

CHAPTER SIX

At Christmas in 1929, the grand entry hall was decorated as it had been in the past, but seventeen year old Nellie was more preoccupied with getting ready to be presented at the annual Christmastime Ball than she was in decorating the tree. I'd witnessed numerous dress fittings in her room and was expected to clean up leftover threads and pins when they were done. She would wear a white gown that, to me, looked like a wedding dress, and even without her hair done up, she looked like a princess.

I would have been lying if I said my stomach didn't flip every time I saw her standing there, looking absolutely beautiful. I'd already accepted the fact that if I ever married, I'd never be able to pay for such finery. *I'd* be the one to marry the grocery delivery man.

On the Saturday before Christmas, I watched as the Fletchers were driven in a horse-drawn carriage to the hotel hosting the gala. The next morning, as I was helping Nellie undress, she told me they'd danced until one in the morning, when they paused for dinner, and then continued dancing until eight in the morning when breakfast was served.

By the time I collected her undergarments, and hung her dress on the outside of her wardrobe door, she'd already climbed in to bed and I could hear faint snoring.

That was the year I turned sixteen, and Franklin Fletcher first entered my room at the top of the stairs.

He knocked lightly, and when I opened my door, he said, "Close the door, lest someone will see me."

He came under the pretext he had another book for me to read.

"But you could have given this to me downstairs," I said, not quite comprehending his intentions.

"Then everyone would have thought I was playing favorites," he said. "Open it."

It was *Lady Chatterley's Lover*.

I'd never thought of Mr. Fletcher in any romantic way, but he was definitely a handsome man and obviously old enough to be my father. That thought, in itself, made me flinch.

I *did* start to read the book though, and found that it aroused in me feelings I had never been aware of. I'd envisioned images of a man and a woman together, but nothing like what I read. He came back a few nights later and when I heard his gentle knock, I didn't answer. I hoped he would go away and forget about me, but that was not to be the case. The next night, he knocked again, and I knew I had to answer.

"You didn't open your door," he said, once inside.

"I didn't know you were there; I'd already fallen asleep," I lied.

"Have you started reading the book?"

"Yes."

"Then you know why I'm here," he said, removing my robe.

His fingers traced around my breasts and down my stomach until he got to my necessities. I noticed he was watching me intently and a glimmer of a smile told me he'd seen how I'd reacted to his touch. There was a tingling in the pit of my stomach.

When he touched me inside, I shivered, and he smiled even wider.

"This is just an idea of what I have in store for you," he said, kissing me on my lips.

And then he left.

I hardly slept that night. Thoughts of being touched, and of the danger of being with Mr. Fletcher, overwhelmed me. If I refused, they could let me go. If I consented, we could be found out and not only would it shame me, but the end result would be the same. I'd be tossed out with nowhere to go.

I know I eventually slept, for I woke to my mother pounding on my door.

"Ruthie, we're going to be late!" She called out. "I swore I heard voices in the night," she said as we descended the stairs. "Did you hear anything?"

"No," I whispered. "I was dead to the world."

That evening, I asked one of the other girls to serve dinner, for I didn't want to have to face Mr. Fletcher. I stayed at the doorway, and I could tell he noticed I wasn't there as he looked around the room. I tended to the meal on the buffet, needlessly rearranging the food and watching for any sign that Mrs. Fletcher could see there was a difference in me. I eventually picked up the dinner plates and silverware, making sure I didn't make eye contact with anyone.

Later that night, he came to my room again, and I had such mixed emotions, I was almost nauseous. Before taking his dinner jacket off, Mr. Fletcher removed my robe again and repeated the gentle touch to my skin. I tried not to gasp as he touched me down there, and I could see I amused him.

He laid me down on my bed and finally undressed. I could see his manhood and I was shocked. I would later wonder why I hadn't expected to see such a sight. He touched me again, making me ready for him, but when he entered me, I gasped in pain. He quickly covered my mouth to silence me. When he was finished, he let out a huge sigh and rolled over.

"Next time, it will be even better for you," he said, putting his clothes back on.

Again, I had a restless night, but was awake early. When I looked at my bed sheet I sickened, for on it were spots of blood. I had no choice but to take them to the laundress, who I worried would know what had happened.

"I had an accident," I said when I handed them to her.

She shrugged her shoulders and set aside the sheet to soak.

Mr. Fletcher came to my room once more before I started my monthly, and as I usually did, I bled on the sheet in the night. My stomach turned cold when I realized I'd have to bring the sheet down to the laundress, knowing she'd question me.

I handed her the sheet and said, "I've had a long period this time."

Had I imagined the scrutiny in her eyes? Did she believe me? Or could she have figured it out about me and Mr. Fletcher?

"Don't worry," she said cheerfully. "I'll get it out."

He came to me once or twice a week after that. What shocked me was that I'd actually grown to look forward to his visits, for he'd done what he promised; he taught me what I thought was passion.

CHAPTER SEVEN

During the summer of 1930, the family planned a cruise from Seattle to Los Angeles. Mrs. Fletcher had family there and they planned on spending two weeks sightseeing.

"I wish you could go with us," Nellie said one afternoon. "We're going to the Natural History Museum where there are dinosaurs, and Father has planned a trip to the movie studios and we'll see Laurel & Hardy and Joan Crawford at the Grauman's Chinese Theatre."

She rattled all this off like she was a child of twelve, hardly taking a breath. I had to admit, I would have loved to have gone with them, but the hierarchy didn't work out. A maid might travel with the family, but they'd never be included in any sightseeing.

Not a week later, everything changed.

"Ruthie," Nellie cried out when she found me in her room. "I've been looking for you everywhere. You'll never believe what's happened?"

"Won't you ever learn to pick up after yourself?" I asked as I picked up a pair of her shoes to put in her wardrobe closet.

"Why should I when I have you? Now listen to me. Father said we could bring you on our trip!"

To say I was speechless was an understatement. There was no way I was going to travel with the family of the man who I laid with.

"Someone will have to stay with the three of us, so it might as well be you."

Once I had a moment to gather my thoughts, I said, "But what will I do all day while you're all out and about?"

"Oh, I'm sure Father can think of something."

"And what will I wear?"

I was going to Los Angeles.

I helped Nellie, Abigail and Francis pack, and the laundress cleaned and pressed several uniforms for me to wear on board and in Los Angeles. I'd had butterflies in my stomach the entire week before we left, and no matter how many times my mother reminded me to relax, I couldn't. On that Monday morning we were to set sail, I watched our luggage being loaded into the car and I wondered if I would get car sick from it all.

Once on board, Mrs. Fletcher made certain I had explicit directions to our cabin before the four of us set off.

"Now you behave for Ruth Ann," she said to the younger ones.

We shared a cramped room one deck below the Fletchers; there was barely enough room for the four of us. Nellie claimed a bottom berth and told me I could have the other one. Abigail and Francis were fine climbing the ladders to the upper beds. We had a washing cabinet between the beds, which provided fresh water for washing our hands and drinking. I unpacked our basics and hung our clothing in the small closet. After that, we found the lavatories down the hallway.

Before we set sail, the four of us went up on deck to watch the ship depart. Someone was passing out streamers, so we each took one; no one had come to see us off, but we waved at all the well-wishers below, anyway. I hadn't ever traveled outside the mansion in my uniform, and I felt self conscious, but I followed along with the other passengers. Oddly, no one gave me the time of day; it was obvious I was the children's maid, and that was that.

Growing bored with it all, Francis wanted to see what else was on deck, so we first discovered the gymnasium with its hours posted; 9:00 – 12:00 pm for ladies, 1:00 – 3:00 for children and 2:00 – 6:00 pm for gentlemen. We watched for a few minutes as an attendant inside was busy setting out towels. Then we came across the swimming pool, the barbershop with the barber inside sharpening his razor against his leather strop, and the first-class lounge with sofas upholstered in plush velvet, and groups of chairs and tables placed around the room. I peeked my head in and to the left saw a fireplace and hundreds of books in the bookcases. An ornate gold framed signboard listed the schedule of upcoming events: tea, coffee and light refreshments at 11:00 am and 3:00 pm, cocktails at 4:00 pm, and after dinner digestifs between 9:00 p.m. – 10:30 p.m.

We were on board for only a few hours when lunch was served. I was told I'd be eating in the main dining room with the other servants, so I accompanied the children (as I still referred to them) to their table with their parents, and as I was about to leave, Mr. Fletcher said, "Good afternoon, Ruth."

"Good afternoon, sir," I said, slightly bowing to him and Mrs. Fletcher.

"I trust you'll enjoy the voyage," he said casually.

I asked the steward where I'd be seated, and he pointed me toward the other side of the room, beyond the ornate candelabras, the richly carved paneling and printed carpets. There were only three tables for maids, and most of them were filled. It was the first time I didn't feel so conspicuous, for everyone was dressed in their various uniforms. Most of them looked like governesses.

There were five of us at my table. To my right was a young girl named Julia, who worked for a family with three children. It was obvious this was the first time she'd been on a ship too, for she was also nervous. On my left, Helena's family also had three children, but they were very young and active. She'd been on one other cruise before this one. Rebecca looked after one child, and Lizzy cared for twins. It was interesting to learn about how they met their families, and when the conversation drifted to how they were treated, most of the women said they were happy for now; they felt their employers were fair with them, especially getting to go on a cruise.

"And especially to be served our meals instead of serving," one girl said.

We all giggled.

Lunch for us consisted of salad, roast beef, vegetables and dessert.

I ate much more than I normally did and was grateful when we finished our meal and I could stand and wait near the family's table for the children.

"I saw a shuffleboard game on deck," Francis was saying to his mother. "Can I have Ruth take me? I don't know how to do it, but I'm sure I'll figure it out."

"What do you think, Franklin?" Mrs. Fletcher asked her husband.

"Hm?"

Mr. Fletcher was cutting the end of his cigar and wasn't paying attention.

"Can Ruth take the children up on the deck?"

"They're not really *children*, Rose Mary. Yes, she can take them on deck. In fact, I might go also, and enjoy my cigar."

"Then, what shall I do?" Mrs. Fletcher asked, crestfallen.

Mr. Fletcher only looked at her.

"Why don't you go to the lounge? I saw a group of women in there earlier; it looks like a place where you can sit and read, or strike up a conversation with someone."

"If that's what you'd like. Go have your cigar then," she said, obviously disappointed.

"Are you ready?" he said to everyone. He gestured for the stewards and within seconds, they were there, pulling out their chairs. Nellie waited a moment for help with hers, but Abigail and Francis pushed their own chairs back and came to where I was standing.

"Can we go now?" Francis asked.

Nellie told me her parents received a formal paper invitation to dine at the captain's table that night, so the children sat at a table near mine, but separated from the servant's section. Not long after they were seated, two more young people were escorted to the table by their serving steward, and given menus. I watched as their parents were seated next to Mr. and Mrs. Fletcher.

In her long evening dress, Mrs. Fletcher looked stunning. She took off the gloves that went to her elbows, and it was the first time I'd seen her with a diamond bracelet. She wore pearls and diamonds at her ears, and her necklace caught the light of the chandelier above them.

Suddenly, I was envious of her. I hadn't been before, but it was so obvious she and I lived in two different worlds. And then I caught the eye of Mr. Fletcher as he looked directly at me, and I froze.

"Are you all right?"

It was my tablemate Julie, and she'd touched my shoulder.

I quickly went back to my menu, and when the steward came to take our orders, I asked for roast turkey and vegetables. Suddenly, I wasn't very hungry.

Although the seas were calm, I was the only one in our cabin to complain of motion sickness, and after having a few crackers, I felt fine.

Our second day at sea was a repeat of the day before, with the exception that we were taken on a private tour of the ship. After breakfast, we spent two hours seeing everything from the galley to the laundry, engine control room, and backstage of the theater. After that, we had lunch, and then I read while Francis and Abigail kept themselves busy. A few times I glimpsed Nellie talking with one young officer or another, and wondered what her father would think of that.

The Fletchers must have been important people, for they received another invitation to dine at the captain's table, but this time with different guests. After that, they'd watched a stage production in the theater. Even though Nellie had pleaded with her father to include me in the entertainment, I was a servant, and not invited.

I made her tell me all about it when they came back to our cabin.

"It was heavenly," Nellie said. "George Gershwin's band played all night, and I danced with anyone who asked. Of course I danced with Father, and even Francis got up to waltz with Mother." She looked away then, as if her head was in the clouds. "I just love to dance. Don't you?"

The night before our last day at sea, I packed us all up and set our luggage outside our door for the porters to pick up. We'd disembarked early the next morning. Mrs. Fletcher's sister, Heloise, was there to greet us, waving from her Cadillac LaSalle limo. Behind her was a Dodge panel truck with a boldly painted P. Larson, Ships Provisions sign on it. The driver piled our luggage inside, and the family crammed into the limo. There was no room for me, but then again, servants rarely got to travel with the family they worked for.

"You can climb in with me," the driver said. "I won't bite."

CHAPTER EIGHT

We stayed in the new Beverly Wilshire Hotel, across the street from an exclusive shopping area called Rodeo Drive. Mrs. Fletcher and her sister spent two days there shopping, bringing home bags of purchases: everything from Gucci to Van Cleef & Arpels. They had their hair done, had lunch in outdoor cafes, and mingled with movie stars. Mr. Fletcher was fitted for a new suit.

Again, I shared a suite with the younger Fletchers, and it was even grander than the mansion in Seattle. Other than the one spot beyond the swimming pool where I could sit and read, I would be confined to our rooms. Mrs. Fletcher didn't want me to accompany the children anywhere, and that's where I'd take my meals.

"Mother said we can order lunch," Nellie said as I unpacked everything.

She'd called down for room service.

About forty minutes later, there was a knock on the door, and I looked at Nellie, wondering if I should answer it.

"Oh, go ahead," she said.

"Room service," a woman's voice called out.

When I opened the door, a young woman smiled and said, "With all this food, you must be hungry."

She wheeled a table over to a dining area and started setting out plates of hamburgers, French fries, and chocolate milkshakes.

"I'm starving," Francis said, deciding which plate was his.

"They're all alike," Nellie said. "Just take one."

"Where are you all from?"

"Seattle, Washington," Nellie said.

"We're here visiting my aunt," Abigail said.

She waited a moment, and then said, "Well, enjoy your lunch."

After she left, Nellie said, "I think she was waiting for her tip, but I don't have any money. I'll have to ask Father for some."

"Oh," was all I said. I'd never heard of tipping.

"Let's go down to the pool," Francis said.

"I'll just stay here," I said. "I think your mother prefers it now that we're here."

Nellie looked at me like I'd just said the most preposterous thing.

"Why would you say that?"

"I heard her saying it to your father."

"Well, that's ridiculous."

"Don't say anything to her. I don't want her being angry with me," I pleaded.

Nellie sighed.

"I'll just clean everything up and read my book while it's quiet."

"Okay."

With that, they got their swimming outfits out and left. It was actually quite nice to have some peace and quiet.

Not ten minutes later, the phone rang. I hesitated, but then answered.

"I saw the children in the lobby."

It was Mr. Fletcher.

"Yes, they've gone to the swimming pool, and I'm here and going to read."

"I'd like to see you."

"I'd feel terribly uncomfortable, Mr. Fletcher, with the children and Mrs. Fletcher being so close."

"I can get us another room."

"I'm also having my monthly," I lied.

"Well, that won't do."

And then he hung up.

I'd been lying to Mr. Fletcher for months, coming up with any excuse I could think of that would turn him away. I was hoping he would stop trying to see me on his own, but nothing I was doing was working. I was not so naïve to think he loved me; even in the beginning when he drew me into his web, I quickly understood this was not love. I tolerated his advances, and for that, I was ashamed. I knew what we were doing was wrong; I'd known it from the very beginning, and if I was honest with myself, I shouldn't have been such a coward. I should have come forward when he first came to me, but I misunderstood the emotions I felt. And I couldn't risk my mother and me losing our jobs. Even worse, no one would have believed me.

In my heart, I knew I was heading toward a dead end, but I wasn't sure how I was going to find the answer to my dilemma. I was going to have to think of something.

"Mother says you can order dinner in the room, but to be careful how much you're spending," Nellie said to me when they returned to the room. "We'll be going down to the dining room and meeting my aunt and uncle."

The dinner menu was extensive and there were no prices listed, so I did not know how much my meal was going to cost. Fearing a tongue-lashing if I made the wrong choices, I ordered a turkey sandwich, cut fruit and a root beer.

The knock at my door told me it was room service, and when I opened the door, I was surprised to see the same young woman.

"Hello, again," she said pleasantly.

"Hello, back," I said.

She pushed the cart to the eating area and uncovered my meal.

"Are you on your own?" she asked. "I'm Charlotte."

"I'm Ruth Ann, but everyone calls me Ruthie. Yes. The children—well, they're not really children—have gone down to have dinner. It's my place to stay here in the room."

"Do you wear your uniform all the time?"

"Yes, that's expected," I said, smoothing out my skirt.

"Hmm," she said. "Of course, I have to wear mine when I work, but I have time off every day."

"So do I, but I live in the house with the family, so I'm always on call if there's an emergency."

"That must be hard."

"I'm used to it. I've been working there since I was ten."

"Ten? Good grief. How old are you now?"

"I'll be seventeen in a month. I've heard some girls eventually leave their families to marry, but I don't have any prospects. And my mother has worked for them for ages."

"What's the family like?"

"Well," I thought for a minute. "I mostly have the children to care for; the missus is okay, I suppose, but she keeps an eye on me. The mister. . .," and here I stopped.

"Oh, my gosh! You've turned absolutely red!" She came to me and touched my arm. "Are you all right?"

Suddenly, I couldn't control myself, and I burst into tears.

"Ruth," Charlotte whispered, comprehension dawning on her.

"I don't know what's come over me," I cried. "I really don't."

"Well, I do. Does anyone know this? Your mother? Anyone in the household?"

"No. And I can't do anything about it or I'll certainly be let go."

"My god, Ruth. This is not good at all."

Charlotte hugged me, and I cried harder.

"We've got to do something about this, before it's too late," she then said. "Let me put my thinking cap on. Will you still be here tomorrow?"

"Yes, we're here for a few more days."

"Here," Charlotte said, handing me a napkin. "Blow your nose and splash cold water on your face so you won't look like you've been crying when they get back. In the meantime, try to eat your dinner. It could be your last one here."

I wasn't quite sure what that meant, so in reply, I just shrugged my shoulders.

Not twenty minutes later, I heard three soft knocks. Thinking it was my new friend again, I quickly opened the door, but instead of Charlotte, there stood Mr. Fletcher.

"Let me in," he said, making his way into the room. "I only have a few minutes. I've told everyone I wanted to make sure you had money to tip your room service."

"Please," I whispered. "This has to stop."

"What did you just say to me?"

The skin between his eyes drew together, and his left eyebrow rose. My stomach felt like it folded in on itself and for a few seconds, I couldn't breathe. But then I took a deep breath for courage and repeated myself.

"No. This has to stop. You've put me in a terrible position, and there's no way out but for me to stop it."

"*Stop?*" he asked with deceptive calm. "*Stop?*"

I stepped back, but he stepped forward. I could not look him in the eye, and I turned to walk away. That's when he twisted my arm and pushed me towards one of the beds. But instead of landing on it, I fell off to the side and landed on the floor.

Suddenly, there was laughter outside the door, and we both heard the turning of the key in the lock.

"Father," Nellie called out in surprise.

"Hello, darling. I just gave Ruth Ann some change for her room service, and it rolled under the bed. She was just looking for it, weren't you, Ruth?"

Nellie looked from her father to me, and although I wanted to tell her the truth. I could see the doubt in her face, and a warning sounded in my brain. I couldn't bear to expose myself or her father.

"Here it is," I said, standing. I pretended to put a coin in my apron pocket.

"Are you asleep?" Nellie asked later as she climbed into our bed.

I knew I'd never truly sleep that night, but I convinced her I was asleep by remaining silent. She quietly asked again, then turned out the lamp on her nightstand and pulled the covers up to her chin. A few minutes later, she turned away from me, on her side, and by her breathing, I could tell she'd fallen asleep.

No matter what I did, no matter how I tossed and turned, I slept fitfully, replaying my life over and over in my mind. And I had to figure a way out.

I was finally sound asleep when Nellie got up. Water from the shower woke me.

"I thought you'd never wake up," she said, wrapping a towel around her hair.

"I don't think I slept well. I feel like I might be coming down with something."

"Why don't you stay in bed, then? We're going shopping with Mother and Aunt Heloise today, so you'll have the room all to yourself."

I was frantic. I ordered room service for breakfast, but it wasn't Charlotte who came to deliver it. My stomach was so upset, I barely ate my toast. At lunchtime, I called for room service again and asked if Charlotte was working.

"I believe she is, ma'am," a woman said.

"Thank you," I replied, hanging up the phone.

Thirty minutes later, there was a knock on my door, and when I opened it, I burst into tears again, for Charlotte stood there. Just seeing her brought a sudden clarity to my situation, and I said, "I have to leave."

I told her about Mr. Fletcher coming to the room, and how I pretended everything was all right when the children saw him there.

"I can't go back," I said.

"Then come with me. I have an idea."

I had nothing to wear but my uniform, so I gathered the few things from the room that were mine, and we left. We brought the food with us. I followed her down the hall and we made our way down to the kitchen.

"Stay here. No one will say anything, and as soon as I'm off, we'll leave," Charlotte said.

My mind raced with images of the children coming back to the room and wondering where I'd gone. The rest of my uniforms were still hanging in the closet, but my underwear and my brush were gone. Would they go to dinner thinking I'd be back when they returned? When they came back and I still wasn't there, would they worry? Would Nellie call her father? And how would he react?

The family and I weren't due to leave for Seattle for a few more days, and while I had no idea where Charlotte was taking me, I worried they'd find me. Should I have left a note? And what would I have said?

On and off, I nibbled at my lunch, then covered it with a towel. I couldn't bear to look at it. Just then, I thought about my mother. What would she do without me? Surely she'd wonder if I was all right, but I didn't see any way I could contact her without the staff finding out. And then, I'd be forcing her to lie about my whereabouts. The worst was, would they make her pay for the uniform I kept?

Once I knew where I was ending up, I'd find a way to reach out to her.

"I have no money," I said as we left the hotel.

"I just got my check, and tomorrow I'll cash it. We'll be okay. I've packed us something for dinner," Charlotte said. "We're going to my apartment for tonight. Then, tomorrow we're going on a trip."

"I have nothing to wear."

"You'll be fine. I have plenty of things you can try on."

She shared an apartment with her friend Clara, who also worked at the hotel.

"Ruthie is coming with us," Charlotte announced when Clara came home. "She's a real servant, and she's run away from her master."

Clara's eyes widened, and I cringed.

"I hope you don't mind," I said awkwardly.

"Any friend of Charlotte's is a friend of mine," Clara said warm-heartedly. And then to Charlotte, "What did you bring for dinner? I'm starving."

We unpacked roast beef, mashed potatoes, vegetables, and some chocolate cake and served ourselves from their small kitchen table. Afterward, we listened to The Lone Ranger and Guy Lombardo's band on the radio, while I tried on several dresses Charlotte handed me. I hadn't worn anything but my uniform for almost eight years, and there was nothing like putting on a soft dress that felt like silk. Clara went through her jewelry box and found a pair of drop earrings for me.

And then she said, "Here, try on this hat."

She handed me a tan felt cloche hat that suited me, except I thought it looked better on them with their short cropped hair.

"You should cut your hair," Clara suggested.

Instinctively, I reached to touch my hair, which for years had been worn in a bun at the back of my neck.

"It would certainly change my look, wouldn't it?" I said, looking in their mirror.

"We can see if there's a shop that can do it when we get there," Charlotte said.

"And that reminds me, where exactly are we going?" I asked.

"You'll see. You'll love it," Charlotte answered. "Try these shoes on. They look like they'll fit you just fine."

They were black T-Bars, with straps that traveled up to meet my ankle, and they fit perfectly. I turned every which way and liked what I saw in the Cheval mirror. Even if the Fletchers saw me, they'd never recognize me.

"And to finish it off, here's a pearl necklace," Charlotte said.

"These aren't real, are they?" I asked, worried.

"Of course not, silly," Clara said.

"Well, I don't know about you two, but I'm tired. And we need to get up early to be ready for the guys," Charlotte said, handing me a set of sheets and a blanket for the couch.

CHAPTER NINE

In the morning, Charlotte and Clara packed a basket with sandwiches and before we went downstairs, Charlotte found a long coat for me to wear. I put it on and looked at myself in the mirror again; I loved the luxury of all my new clothes, even if they might just be temporary. We waited a few minutes, and when their friends, Finn and Miles drove up in a Model A four-door sedan, the three of us girls crammed into the back seat like canned sardines.

We drove for two hours before we turned on to Waterman Canyon, a narrow winding road leading up a mountainside. We immediately saw the mountainside. The contrasting vegetation that framed what was a near perfect arrowhead looked like it had been carved into the mountain.

"It's pointing to the hot springs," Charlotte said.

"Where are we?" I finally asked.

"You'll see."

We pulled into a turnout that overlooked the valley below and parked the car. Finn and Miles got out first and stretched, then they opened our doors and took the picnic basket to a table. Finn got thermoses and mason jars from the chest on the fold down luggage rack, while Charlotte and Clara set out our lunch.

"French 75 anyone?" Finn asked, pouring a gin and champagne mixture into our drink jars.

A little over two miles up the hill, Finn turned right onto a dirt road and we created quite a bit of dust. I was glad we weren't in an open car, or I would have been sneezing my head off. We came upon a twenty-five foot wide arched entry built of granite boulders and a sign that said "Arrow Head." A statue of an Indian pointed the way.

Up ahead stood a magnificent white hotel, and as we drove closer, we could see cars waiting in line to let off their passengers. Uniformed bellhops greeted them and took their luggage up the steps to the lobby. We weren't planning on staying at the hotel, so we bypassed the parking attendants and found a spot in the shade not too far from the entrance.

"We'll go in acting like we belong here," Miles said, leading the way. He took Clara's arm, and they walked ahead of us.

To the left, guests waited two deep at the reservation station, and to our right, more guests sat in clusters of sofas and chairs and were deep in conversation.

"Have you been here before?" I asked no one in particular.

"Oh yes," Charlotte said. "We've come here and had drinks on the outdoor patio. It's fun to pretend we have the money to stay here, and no one even bothers to question us."

Miles pulled chairs out so we could sit around a table that had a large umbrella coming from the center. No sooner had we sat, then an attendant, complete with a white bar towel draped over his arm, stood awaiting our order.

"We'll all have French 75s," he said confidently.

"Certainly, sir."

"We'll have one drink, and then we can walk to the hot springs," Charlotte said. "You'll be amazed at how warm the water is."

Once we headed towards the springs, a smell of rotten eggs filled the air.

"*What is that?*" I asked, plugging my nose.

"It's the hot springs," Miles said. "It's the minerals."

"Phew," I said. "I wouldn't want to soak in something that smells so bad."

But there were ten or twelve people in various stages of either getting in or out of the water or sitting in it waist deep.

Done with our tour, Charlotte pulled me aside and said, "You know, this might be a perfect place for you to get a job. I've heard famous actors like Charlie Chaplin, Buster Keaton, and even Marion Davies and William Randolph Hearst come to stay. We should ask the manager to speak with someone."

"Oh, I don't know..." I started.

"Well, you can't go back now," Charlotte reminded me. "Let's go," she said to the others as she grabbed my hand and literally pulled me towards the patio entrance to the lobby. "Let me find out who you can talk to."

A few minutes later, we were standing in front of the head housekeeper, Mrs. Schmidt.

"Well, you look presentable enough," she said, tilting her head. "And you say you've been a maidservant for eight years? You must have started when you were a baby."

"Yes ma'am," I said. "I mean, no ma'am. I was ten."

"And why aren't you serving the family now?" she asked.

"Well."

"They no longer needed her to be in charge of the children. They've all grown up," Charlotte said quickly.

"I see."

"We're on our way up to Lake Arrowhead right now to answer an ad for help."

"I see," Mrs. Schmidt said. "Well, let me look in my book to see what we have." With this, she sat back down at her desk and opened a record book. With one finger, she went line by line, reading name after name, before she looked up.

"I think we might have something for you, then. Do you have a place to stay?"

"Not yet, ma'am. I'm just newly from Seattle," I said.

"Hmm," she said thoughtfully. "I believe we have a shared room that's available. Can you get along with a fellow member of the staff?"

"I'm sure I can, ma'am."

Mrs. Schmidt's mouth twisted in thought.

"If you'd like, we can check back in after we make it up to Arrowhead. Ruth will know then where she'd rather work," Charlotte said.

"There's not another place like this up here, so I know she'll do better here."

I worried Charlotte had pushed it and then she said, "It was very nice to meet you, Mrs. Schmidt." She extended her hand, but Mrs. Schmidt didn't take it.

"You can have the job, then. The pay is fifty cents an hour, minus five dollars a month for your room. And you can start the day after tomorrow."

I floated out of there.

We found the others outside by the car. Miles had just lit a cigarette and wanted to finish it before we took off.

"How'd it go?" he asked.

"I got the job!" I blurted. "Or, rather, Charlotte got me the job!"

"Well, she had to have liked you or no matter what I said, she wouldn't have hired you."

"Still," I said, hugging her. "I don't know how I can ever thank you."

"Buy me an ice cream when we get to Lake Arrowhead."

"It's a deal."

As we climbed the winding road up the mountain, I could hear the strain of Finn's engine, and I hoped we wouldn't end up stranded somewhere. Thankfully, there weren't a lot of cars on the road, going either up or down the narrow road, but I still worried we'd end up going over the side of the road, tumbling down to our deaths. The sudden reeling from one side to the other when Finn didn't anticipate the bends in the road was making me slightly nauseous, plus sitting between Charlotte and Clara meant one or the other of them was always leaning into me.

I didn't know if it was the alcohol I'd drunk or the heat, but I knew if we didn't stop the car I was going to throw up.

"I need you to pull over at the next spot," I said. "I think I'm going to be sick."

"Hell's bells," Finn said. "Hang on there."

"Breathe deeply," Charlotte said.

Thankfully, we came to a turnout, and we pulled over. Clara opened her door, and it wasn't too soon. Before I got all the way out, I threw up.

"Yowza!" Finn said.

The bile from the gin and champagne was bitter in my mouth. Charlotte got out and got some napkins from the picnic basket and came to me.

"Are you all right?"

"I think I am now. I've never driven on such a winding road before. And I do feel better. I'm so sorry," I said.

"I brought a jug of water in case I needed it for the radiator. It's in the chest if you want some," Finn called out from the front seat.

"That would be wonderful."

Fortunately, for the rest of the trip, Clara let me sit by the window, and I drifted off to sleep. I woke as we drove into a small town and pulled in to a gravel entrance to a series of log cabins. We were all ready to stretch our legs and the fresh air invigorated me. The afternoon had cooled off, and I took in a deep breath and closed my eyes. I could feel *and* hear the wind blowing in the trees, and then I heard a slight crunching sound. When I opened my eyes and looked up, I saw the cutest squirrel looking down on me, casually munching on something he held between his two front paws.

Miles and Charlotte came out of the one cabin that had a carved wood "Office" sign hanging by the door, and when Miles said, "The guys get one cabin, and the girls get the other," it startled the squirrel and he quickly climbed to a higher branch.

The afternoon air had turned chilly, and I remembered my coat was still in the car.

"Does anyone need anything?" I called before I closed the car door.

"Bring my coat too," Charlotte said.

Our cabins were small, but better than anywhere else I'd stayed, except for the hotel in Los Angeles. The walls were made of logs, and the fireplace took up one wall. There was one bed, which Charlotte and Clara would share, and Miles brought in a cot for me. He put some logs on the grate, then rolled up some old newspapers and lit them to get the fire started.

"You girls will have to make sure the fire is lit during the night, so you don't freeze," he said. "I'll bring in more wood from the porch."

We'd finished putting our things away, and when it started getting dark, I wondered about dinner. I was hungry, and relieved when Finn knocked on our door and asked, "Is anyone else hungry?"

"I am," Clara said.

We found a small diner down the road and ordered two roast beef meals for the five of us to share. Our waitress gave us a stern look when we asked for another basket of bread and butter to help fill us up.

"Will you be having dessert, then?" she asked as she took away our plates.

"I'm full," Miles said. "What about you girls?"

I knew no one was too full to pass up dessert, but since I had no money, I couldn't very well suggest it.

"I'm good," we all said at once.

"I saw a corner store before we got here. What say we stop in there and get some cookies and sodas?" Miles said.

When we got back to the cabins, Miles and Finn pulled chairs into a circle around a fire pit.

"These are like the chairs we saw at the hotel," I said. "They look clunky, but the way they slant back makes them comfortable; even if they're made of wood."

The boys gathered wood and lit the fire, and we all sat as close as we could so we could feel the warmth. In the dark, our faces were illuminated, and Charlotte said, "Why don't we tell ghost stories?"

I hated the idea, but Miles started. As he spoke, I could hear the tree branches move, and I swore I heard a rustling in the bushes in front of us. I knew it wasn't ladylike, but I pulled my knees up to my chest, and wrapped myself in my coat.

"Something's out there," I whispered.

Miles stopped talking and looked from side to side. Then he howled like a dog, and we all jumped. He and Finn cracked up. But then the bushes rustled again, and they stopped laughing. We all watched in silence, and then we cried out as a dog came running out to where we were.

"Mabel," Mr. Maynard, the cabin owner, yelled. "Git over here! You liked to scare these kids half to death!" He gently grabbed her by the collar and pulled her towards him. "Sorry about that. She's out for her evening constitutional. Now don't you kids forget to put dirt over the fire when you're ready to hit the sack. We don't want no forest fires here."

The next morning, Miles and Finn borrowed a couple of fishing poles from Mr. Maynard. He told them about a campground where there were plenty of fish, but they promised to take us to the village first. They patiently waited outside for us while we made our way through all the stores. The first place we stopped at was the Candyland Candy Store, and it was filled with more types of candy than I'd ever imagined; when Charlotte said she'd treat me to a piece, I had a difficult time deciding what to buy.

There was a haberdashery called Brooks Brothers, with button-down shirts, silk ties and suits. A store filled with preserves and cheeses smelled absolutely delicious when we walked in, but the prices they were asking were outrageous. There was a tea store, a lady's clothing store, and I died and thought I'd gone to heaven when I stepped in to the bookshop, called Books & Co. I ran my fingertips over rows and rows of new books, and then in the back of the store, the woody smell of used books filled the air. I closed my eyes and took a deep breath. And then I saw a copy of *The Swiss Family Robinson*!

I pulled it to my chest and could have cried.

"May I help you?" asked a stout older man who must have been the bookseller.

"Oh," I started. "I can't believe I've found this. I lost my copy..."

"How much is it?" Charlotte asked as she came to stand beside me.

"It's one dollar," he said.

"I'll get it for you," Charlotte said, looking through her purse.

"I can't let you do that. I don't know how I'll ever pay you back for what you've done for me already."

"It's my treat," she said.

I didn't know what to say, so I just stood there, holding on to my first book since starting over.

We drove around the lake until we found the beach on the north shore. Miles and Finn unloaded the basket filled with the sandwiches we'd made, then they headed for the wooden dock where they set up to fish. The three of us set up our lunch on the picnic table opposite the dock. There, we sat first at the table, until we saw the same type of chairs that were at the cabins. We basked in the warm sun. I'd only brought one change of clothes, and the same cloche hat helped shield my face from getting burned.

About an hour later, the guys came back with four fish, and Charlotte asked, "How will you keep them from smelling? We don't have a way to cook them, and I don't even like fish."

"We'll give them to Mr. Maynard. He'll find a use for them," Miles said.

By the time we'd finished our lunch, I could feel my skin growing tender and pink, and I was ready to leave. Once we packed everything up, we kept driving the road around the lake until we made our way back to the cabins. Mr. Maynard was delighted to get the fish, and once Mabel sniffed the bucket and determined she wasn't interested, she followed him into the office.

"I'll have it tonight," Mr. Maynard said, turning to face us. Then he turned to me. "Did you ladies have a good day?"

I turned beet red, but Charlotte answered, "We did."

Once inside our cabin, she said, "I think he has eyes for you."

"Oh, don't be silly. He's older than Mr. Fletcher, who is old enough to be my father."

The thing about Mr. Maynard was, the few times I'd seen him, he didn't have any of the characteristics that Mr. Fletcher did. He didn't give me the impression he had to be in control at all times, he loved his dog, and he had a nice smile. But he was old.

Not long after that, we left to make our way back down the hill where I could be dropped off at the hotel. I started work the next morning, so I wanted some time to get settled.

"I had a wonderful time," I said as we grew closer.

"That was the plan," Charlotte said, squeezing my hand. "You deserve a much better life than what you had, and I think you'll find it here."

"How will I get the dress back to you? And how will I repay you for the book?"

"Consider them my gift to you. If a friend can't help another friend, then what are they good for?"

"I hope we see each other again," I said, and as hard as I tried, I couldn't stop the tears from filling my eyes.

"You'll be fine. Here's my address," she said, writing it on a piece of paper. "Let me know how you're doing, and assuming you can get mail, I'll let you know if we plan another trip up. How does that sound?"

"I can't thank you enough, Charlotte," I said.

We pulled into the driveway to the hotel, and Miles pulled in under the canopy to let me off. When a bellman came to open my door, Miles got out and said, "We've got it."

I gave him a quick hug and said, "Thank you for bringing me along."

"I'm glad you had a good time."

He honked as they drove away.

CHAPTER TEN

I found Mrs. Schmidt, and she showed me to my room. My new room-mate, Gloria, was already there, and when the door opened, she quickly stood, her body erect, and both her arms were at her sides.

"I need to remind you of the rules," Mrs. Schmidt said. "No men, no gossip, no communicating with the guests except to say 'yes, ma'am or no, sir.' You'll say 'please' and 'thank you' but these are rules you'd already know from working in service. The guest is always right, and your job is to provide the means for them to have a pleasant stay."

"Yes, ma'am," I said.

When she left, Gloria relaxed and smiled at me weakly.

"She doesn't like me," she said.

"Oh," was all I could think of saying.

"She had to hire me because my father works here as the concierge. And she's always finding fault with what I do. But here's your bed. Put your things away and make yourself at home."

My uniform was hanging in the armoire we would share, along with white stockings and black shoes.

"Did the old battleaxe tell you what you'd be doing?"

"No, so I guess I'll find out when I meet with her in the morning."

"I work in the spa. I help guests get in and out of the hot springs, and then I tidy up after massages. Sometimes it's impossible to be in two places at once, but that's what they expect."

"Have you seen movie stars?" I asked.

"Of course, silly. They're all over the place. Most of them are nice to the staff, but some are rude and they talk to us like we're slaves. We're not to talk with them unless they need help or have a question."

"What do you do then?"

"We say 'yes, ma'am' and 'no, ma'am.'"

"The staff showers and toilets are down the hall," Gloria continued. "The hours for men and women are posted. We can use the toilets any-time, but never the ones in the main hotel."

I changed into Charlotte's sleeping clothes, then crawled into bed. I was exhausted from the day, and my skin still felt pink and warm from the sun. I lit the lamp on my nightstand, and opened my book. I planned on only reading until I was sleepy, but within minutes I drifted off to sleep.

I was to work cleaning rooms. Every day we changed bed linens and brought in clean towels, and after check-out the in-room bathrooms were cleaned from head to toe, and the carpets were swept. I worked in tandem with another girl, Sofia, and by the end of each day, we av-eraged cleaning twelve rooms. When we finished our day, we gathered all the laundry, some of it repulsively dirty, and wheeled it down to the washing room. By the time I had dinner and got back to my room, I was dog-tired. My feet were killing me and every muscle I had ached. In the morning, we'd be back loading our cart with enough linens to start all over.

Sometimes, our guests would leave us small tips, and Sofia and I shared them. Sometimes they left sweets and other edible items, but I didn't feel comfortable eating leftovers from someone I didn't know. One time, a guest left a book on their dresser, and instead of telling Sofia, I put it in my pocket. Of course, if they left jewelry or other valuables, we called Mrs. Schmidt and she would come and pick everything up to put in the hotel safe.

Around two weeks after I started working, I got a letter from Charlotte, asking how I was adjusting, and she told me she'd delivered room service to the Fletcher's when she got back and they were terribly worried about me.

"Of course, I never let on that I had any idea where you were," she wrote. "Nellie was the most worried. Her mother told her good riddance. You were right. She probably knew something was up with you and her husband. Didn't you tell me that years ago, another servant was let go because she was pregnant? It was probably him."

I wrote back, letting her know I'd settled in, and I actually enjoyed living in the hotel. The staff was cordial, and I'd already been able to set aside some money. It was wonderful hearing from her and while I hadn't known her all that long, I missed having her as a friend.

Around the fourth week I was at the hotel, I must have eaten something bad, for I woke up the morning after, and felt sick to my stomach. I had eaten with Gloria and a couple of other girls, and no one else had felt the queasiness I had. It went away, and I was fine for the rest of the day. But the next morning, I felt the same way, and while we were cleaning a guest room, I rushed to the toilet and threw up.

"Do you feel all right?" Sofia asked when I came out of the bathroom.

She looked at me like I had a third eye, and throughout the day, she kept asking me if I was okay.

"I'm fine. I must have a bug," I said.

But the next morning, I did the same, and Gloria said, "Not that it's any of my business, Ruthie, but have you been with a man?"

At first I denied it, but when I was sickly during the day, I began to worry. When Sofia asked me the same question, I told her about Mr. Fletcher.

"It can't be. It's been almost two months."

But then I realized I hadn't had my monthlies. I had no idea what being pregnant felt like, and I suddenly realized the seriousness of the predicament I was in.

"What am I going to do? I'll surely be fired," I said, starting to cry. "And I have no place to go."

I wrote to Charlotte, telling her about my situation, and she immediately wrote back.

"You'll certainly lose your job when they find out. I would work as long as you can to save up some money, then either tell them you're moving back home, or let them figure it out and fire you. As far as *where* you'll go, you can't really come back to Los Angeles; the hotel will never hire you if you're pregnant.

"I have a crazy idea," she continued. "When the time comes, why don't you go back up to Lake Arrowhead? Mr. Maynard would probably let you stay in one of the cabins until you can figure out what to do. He was very nice to us, and I told you I thought he had an eye for you."

How could I write back and tell Charlotte I thought that was a terrible idea? I didn't want to live in the mountains, and I didn't want Mr. Maynard feeling sorry for me. *And* I didn't want to be pregnant!

A few days later, when I was taking a bag of linens down to the washing room, I observed a young man I later learned was named Harold, who was unloading bags of laundry washing soap and lye. I could tell they were heavy by the way he made a huffing sound as he neatly stacked each bag in the corner. An idea was brewing.

"Good morning, Harold," I said.

He looked up and wiped his forehead with his shirtsleeve.

"Good morning, miss."

"I've seen you here a few times—how often do you make your delivery?"

I knew I sounded bold in starting a conversation with him, but I didn't care.

"Well," he said. "I deliver soap, lye and bleach every Tuesday, and then on Thursdays I bring up tea, coffee, sugar, flour and rice."

"That must be hard work," I said.

"Well, it isn't, really. And it's a good job."

"Do you deliver to anywhere else?"

"As a matter of fact, I do. I deliver to the big hotel in Lake Arrowhead the same days."

"I see."

"Is there something you need, miss?" he asked.

"No. No. I just find your work very interesting."

"No one's ever said that before," Harold said. He grinned and straightened his shoulders.

"Well, maybe I'll see you again one of these weeks," I said. "You're always here around the same time, then?"

His face brightened at the suggestion.

"Pretty close to it. I have to make it up the hill and back down before it gets dark."

"Well, maybe I'll see you in the next few weeks," I said, dropping my bag into the laundry cart.

"You'd better tell Mrs. Schmidt," Gloria said to me one morning, as we were getting ready to start work. "You're showing more."

"I know. I'm trying to figure out the best time to say something. If I quit, will I get my pay?"

"I don't know; I've never quit. I think when they fire you, they pay you then and there."

"Maybe I'll do that then. Go see her about something and let her make the connection."

As if she read my mind, Mrs. Schmidt called me in to her office that next afternoon.

"Although I've had some positive comments on your work, there's something I need to discuss with you." And then she got right to the point. "I've noticed you're uniform is getting rather tight. Which leads to only two conclusions. One is that you're getting fat, or ..." and she paused. "You're with child. Which is it?"

She didn't let me answer before she said, "Is it someone in the hotel? We have rules, you know, and you've obviously broken them." With this comment, she crossed her arms over her chest.

"No, it wasn't someone from the hotel."

"Well, then."

I decided to tell her the truth.

"I didn't realize I was pregnant when I applied for the job."

"But didn't you say you worked for a family before you came here?"

"Yes, I did."

"Well, then," she said again, drawing her own conclusions.

"I'm very sorry, Mrs. Schmidt. I really liked working here."

"We cannot have you here. Here's your pay for the week," she said, handing me an envelope.

She'd obviously come to this conclusion prior to seeing me. I took the envelope and thanked her.

"Technically, you cannot stay here tonight since you are no longer an employee. Do you have a place to go?"

"No," I said, quietly.

"Well, then. That's not my concern, is it?"

I didn't tell Gloria I'd been fired, mostly because I didn't want her to tell me I couldn't stay in our room that night. I waited until the next morning and told her when we got up. I dressed in the dresses Charlotte gave me, complete with my fake pearl necklace and cloche hat, and made my way out the back entrance. If anyone from the hotel saw me, I hoped they'd think I was just a lost guest.

It was a Thursday, and I made myself inconspicuous as I waited for Harold's truck. I would either hide inside while he was making his delivery, or I would be honest with him and beg him for a ride back up to Lake Arrowhead. I hadn't decided when I saw him drive up.

"Hello, Harold," I said as I stood beside the back of his truck.

"Oh," he said, clearly startled. I could tell he didn't recognize me in regular clothing, but then I saw a flicker of recognition and he grinned. "Well, hello."

"So..." I said as I smiled, slightly suggestively. Then I turned serious. "I've lost my job, and I need a ride up the mountain," I blurted.

Caught again unawares, Harold coughed and cleared his throat.

"Oh, I don't know, miss," he said. "I could probably lose my job too if anyone found out."

"Well, they wouldn't, because I'd hide while you did your delivery, and then walk up the driveway and you could pick me up past the entrance to the hotel."

Harold contemplated that idea, and nodded his head, understanding. A half hour later, I was standing by the Indian statue at the entrance to the hotel, and when Harold saw me, he stopped the truck. I only had a pillowcase as a bag, and I tossed it in before I climbed up.

"Well, where to?" he asked.

"I don't want to take you far from where you're going for your delivery, but there are some cabins I stayed in with my friends. I think I can find them again once we get up there."

"Alrighty, then. Hold on."

About an hour later, we were passing roads that looked familiar, but I didn't recognize any of them as the ones Miles had turned on to. We got to the main road into town.

"Let me know if this looks familiar," Harold said.

"It does. Oh. We ate in that diner. Now let me think."

"Well, I need to get this delivery made, so why don't we do that, and then on the way back, you can let me know if you recognize anything."

We made a turn onto another main road, and by then I was totally lost. Thank goodness Harold knew his way to the hotel, and once we got there, I waited in the truck while he unloaded his delivery.

He took a slightly different route back, and then suddenly, we were at a five-way stop that looked familiar.

"I recognize this road. Turn to the right, and I think the cabins are just down the road."

A few minutes later, there they were. Harold turned right on to the gravel driveway. Mr. Maynard was on both knees, weeding the flower bed in front of the office, and he turned to see who was there.

I jumped out of the truck and called to him. "Mr. Maynard. It's Ruth Ann. I was here a while back with my friends." I waved, even though I was only about ten feet away from him. A sweet woody fragrance filled the air, and I could tell the air was fresher and crisper than it was when I was last there.

His smile widened with recognition. For an older man, he was handsome, with dark eyes. His sleeves were rolled up, and with dirty hands, he wiped perspiration from his forehead, leaving behind a smudge of dirt. Suddenly, his dog Mabel was barking, then jumping on me, wagging her tail with enthusiasm. I felt like I'd just returned home.

"Before I leave you," Harold said, "let's make sure you have a place to stay."

"You're back with us?" Mr. Maynard said.

"Yes, if you have a cabin."

"Well, I sure do."

This was enough for Harold, who jumped back up into his truck and reversed it out on to the road back.

"Thank you," I called out.

He waved back at me without turning.

CHAPTER ELEVEN

Mr. Maynard wiped his hands on his pants, and we went inside the office. Mabel's claws clicked on the wood floor, and she pushed my hand
to pet her. At least *she* was happy to see me.

"How long are you here for?"

"I'm not sure. I'm moving up here, so I'd say as long as it takes me
to find a job and get a place."

"You're here by yourself? Where are your friends?"

"Oh, they went back to Los Angeles. They're from there. I'm originally from Seattle and I met them in L.A."

"Hmm."

"It's okay if it's just me, isn't it? I have the money to pay you."

"Oh, it's not what I was thinking. It was that you came up here by
yourself. Where've you been?"

"I had a job at the hotel on the main road."

"I see. Well," Mr. Maynard said as he ran a finger through his
guest book.

"Oh," I said. "I forgot to ask how much it would cost."

I realized then I should have asked that question before Harold left
me there, but it was too late.

"Well, you said you needed a job, too?"

"Yes. I cleaned the rooms at the hotel. I could do just about anything."

"Well, I could use someone part time, when we have guests, if that would work. Then you could see if you can find anything in town. Somebody's bound to be hiring, I reckon."

I waited for him to tell me an amount, and finally he said, "How's about five dollars a month?"

I knew Mr. Maynard's offer was beyond believable, and I squared my shoulders to prepare for what would come next. Were there going to be expectations of me that I wouldn't be able to abide by? Would he be another Mr. Fletcher who felt he owned me?

"Have I said something to offend you?" Mr. Maynard asked, his face filled with confusion.

He took a few steps closer to me, and Mabel took this as a sign to jump on me again and lick my face.

"Mabel. Stop!" Mr. Maynard said.

She licked me again, this time, on the lips.

"Yuck," I cried out. And then I laughed.

"I'm sorry," he said, gently pulling Mabel away. "Stop. She doesn't want your kisses."

But then I thought, maybe I did.

"I'd like to stay," I said.

I had almost two hundred dollars, and I quickly calculated that it could get me by until I had my baby, even if I didn't find a job.

"Well, good then. Let's get you set up," Mr. Maynard said. "I'll just go get your key."

Mabel followed us to cabin one, and as Mr. Maynard tried a couple of keys, she sniffed at my bag of clothing.

"There's nothing much there, girl," I said.

"I'll show you how to light the fire. It gets chilly in the evenings."

Mr. Maynard filled the grate with logs, then pointed to a stack of old newspapers.

"All you have to do is roll one of those up and hold it for a few seconds to get it started."

He looked at my pillowcase. "Is that all you brought?"

"Yes," I said, embarrassed. "I'll need to buy some clothes somewhere. I'll also need a place to eat, since I'm starving."

"The mountain air will do that to you," he said.

I was sure it would, but I knew it didn't have anything to do with the air.

"I have to go into town tomorrow if you want me to take you somewhere. You'd have time to find some clothes, and then I have to go to the grocer's anyway. What do you say?"

"Oh, I hate to bother you," I started.

"Why, it's no bother at all. As long as you don't mind Mabel here sittin' with us in the truck. Plus, it'll set the town a talking, me coming in with a pretty young woman."

Mr. Maynard gave me a mischievous smile, and I couldn't help but smile back.

I had every intention of sitting in front of the fire and reading the book I'd brought with me from the hotel. It was *The Adventures of Sherlock Holmes*, and I'd never read a mystery novel, so I was eager to see if I liked it. However, exhaustion won out, and instead I fell asleep in the chair. When I woke in the middle of the night, the fire had burned down, and I put more logs in, and then climbed under the thick covers of my bed. I hadn't closed the curtains, and through my window I could see the full moon surrounded by thousands of tiny stars. I sighed deeply, thinking I'd made it this far—but I still had to figure out the rest of my life.

CHAPTER TWELVE

"Mr. Maynard," I said when I saw him the next morning. "How long would it take me to walk to the Village?"

"It's way too far for you to walk. I told you I had errands to do, so I can easily drop you off if you'd like. And will you call me Jack?"

"If it wouldn't be too inconvenient, that would be great. When I was up here with my friends, I found a wonderful bookshop, and I'd love to see if they have anything new to read."

"The feed store is on the way and I need to get Mabel some food, so we can stop there, too."

I grabbed my coat, and we headed to town.

"Now, no kisses today," I said to Mabel as I climbed into the front seat.

She kissed me anyway, and I couldn't help but laugh.

We stopped at the feed store first, and since I'd never been in one, I got out to see what all they had to sell. It smelled like a mixture of hay, birdseed, and dog food. I was surprised it wasn't an unpleasant combination.

"What do you feed the deer or squirrels?" I asked.

"Normally, we don't feed them anything," Mr. Maynard said. "Their job is to find their own food, and truthfully, if we fed the wild animals, they would become more comfortable around humans, and that's not always a good idea. It takes away their natural instincts."

"Oh."

"But sometimes I do buy birdseed for the birds that come around. We have some of the most beautiful Steller's jays."

Once finished, we headed towards the Village.

"I have some guests coming in this weekend, so if you want to go with me to the bakery, I'll pick up some muffins."

Again, my senses were overwhelmed with the aroma of baked goods, and even though I'd had a piece of bread with butter on it for breakfast, my mouth watered. I couldn't help but look at all the rolls and muffins, and when Mr. Maynard asked me if I wanted anything, I told the clerk I'd love to have a cinnamon roll. I reached into my purse to pay for it, and Mr. Maynard said, "It's on me. After all, you're a guest in the cabins."

He turned and winked at me, and I could feel myself color.

After that, I asked him if he had more errands to do in the Village while I went into the bookshop, and he said he hadn't been in there for ages and was interested to see what they had.

The bookshop owner, a Mr. Barlowe, greeted us as we came in.

"Good morning, Jack," he said to Mr. Maynard. "The leaves will be turning soon."

"Clyde, I think you're right. This here is Ruth Landry. She's new up here and loves to read."

"Good morning, Miss Landry."

"Please call me Ruth."

"Okay then. Please call me Clyde. What can I help you with?"

"I was in a couple of months ago, with some friends, and I bought a book," I said, then felt silly thinking he might remember me. "I'm hoping to find something else."

"Well, we have plenty to choose from. Make yourself at home, and let me know if I can help you."

"Thank you," I said as I headed to the back of the store.

Even though he'd asked me to call him Clyde, I felt uncomfortable addressing an older gentleman by his first name. Clyde and Mr. Maynard chatted amiably while I made my way to the row of the older, less expensive used books. I found three I liked: *The Sound and the Fury* by William Faulkner, *The Age of Innocence* by Edith Wharton, and several books by Agatha Christie.

I had the money to buy all three, but I needed to learn to budget, so I brought all three to a table and set them down. I closed my eyes, and said, "Eeny, meeny, miny, moe," as I pointed to each book.

"Ruth, what on earth are you doing?" Mr. Maynard asked, coming to stand next to me.

"Oh," I said, instantly embarrassed. "I'm trying to decide which two books to buy. Am I keeping you?"

"No, we're fine."

I took the William Faulkner and Edith Wharton books to the counter and said, "I'll take these two."

"That'll be two dollars."

"Thanks, and I'll be back."

"See you then," Clyde said.

Once we got back into the truck, I brought the two books to my nose and breathed in their woody smell.

"I love the way old books smell," I said.

Mabel smelled them too, then licked my face.

When we got back to the cabins, Mr. Maynard showed me how to refill the bird feeders. One was attached to the post of the office porch, and two more hung from lower pine tree branches.

"We take a risk of the squirrels getting into these," he said, taking the roofs of the feeders off. "I made these myself. With this wire, it helps, but I've also known bears to knock them down. Now, pour this in," he said, touching my hand. "Not all the way to the top, but pretty far up there."

"How do they know they're here?" I asked. "Do they smell the food?"

"Birds are smart and they have amazing eyesight. They find newly filled feeders listening to other birds and once they find new sources of food in their territory, they keep coming back to see if there's more."

I watched Mr. Maynard as he concentrated on putting the feeders back up, and I watched his muscled forearms and quick fingers. When he turned to me, it caught me off guard. I could tell I'd reddened, and I would have died if he knew what I'd been thinking. He was a kind man, and I truly appreciated the time he was spending with me.

"Although I said we don't usually feed the animals up here, I *have* been known to throw a few acorns and walnuts on the ground around the trees. And I've bought apples for the deer. I've never seen one come eat any, but they're always gone the next time I check."

"Have you ever seen a bear?"

"Not up close, thankfully. I've seen plenty of trash cans knocked over, especially since people throw their food in them."

"I'd love to see a deer, but I can live without seeing a bear," I said.

CHAPTER THIRTEEN

The next time we went into town, I stopped in at a thrift store and bought two dresses and a sweater. While Mr. Maynard shopped at the grocers, I checked the bulletin board and saw there was a help wanted ad for a housekeeper. I quickly jotted the phone number down before Mr. Maynard saw me, and then I wondered what all the secrecy was about. I'd told him I'd be looking for a job. If I could clean one or two houses a week, I'd be all right until I couldn't work any longer.

When we got back to the cabins, I asked if I could use his phone to call about the ad. He stood there while I dialed, then went into the room off the office, which was where he stayed.

A woman answered the phone, and when I told her what I was calling for, she said, yes, she was still looking for someone. It would be two days a week, and when I told her I didn't have a car, she said her driver could pick me up and bring me back home. It paid two dollars per day, and it was cleaning and laundry.

"I'd love to meet you," I finally said. "I'm interested."

"I'll have Patrick come get you. Shall we say tomorrow around noon? I'll be up and ready by then."

"That would be great. I'll see you then."

I wasn't sure what to wear for the interview, so I wore one of my new dresses, including the cloche hat. I knew I was overdressed for a housekeeper interview, and I hoped if I got the job, if it required a uniform, one would be provided.

The next morning at eleven thirty, a fancy car pulled up in the driveway. I hadn't told Mr. Maynard about the job possibility; I wanted to wait and see if I got it first. I saw him peek out his office window, and I waved.

Not long afterward, we pulled into a large circular driveway, and there stood one of the most incredible homes I'd ever seen. It looked like a lodge, and it was right on the edge of the lake.

Patrick opened my door, and directed me to the front door where I lifted a heavy door knocker and rapped three times. A woman in a white uniform came to the door and when I told her who I was, she opened the door wide for me and stepped aside. She directed me to a small room off the entry where I sat and waited.

"Ruth?" a woman's said as she came into the room.

I jumped to my feet. "Yes, ma'am."

"Well, don't you look lovely, all dressed up?"

"Thank you, ma'am."

"My name is Vivian Hayes. I'm sure you've heard of me."

Her name didn't ring a bell, but I could tell she expected me to acknowledge her.

"Why, yes, ma'am," I said.

"I should have put in the ad that I'll only be in the mountains for four more months before I start a new movie, so that would be the duration of your employment."

"I understand," I said, but I was disappointed. I mentally counted the months of my pregnancy and that would bring me to about seven months. No one would want me then.

"Good, then. You said you had experience when we talked on the phone?"

"Yes, ma'am. I worked for a family for almost eight years." I didn't want to mention the hotel, for fear she'd asked me why I was no longer there.

"That should work for me. I'd like you to do the laundry on Mondays, and clean on Thursdays. Maria will show you around the house, so you'll be familiar with the rooms. Patrick will pick you up and take you back home. I'll pay you once a week. Does that suit you?"

"Yes, ma'am. It suits me fine."

"Good, then. We'll start tomorrow."

And with that, Vivian Hayes turned and left the room.

"Oh, ma'am," I called out.

When Miss Hayes returned, I asked, "Will there be a uniform?"

"Yes," she said, and walked away.

The minute Patrick dropped me off at the cabins, I rushed into the office to tell Mr. Maynard about my good luck. Unless I read him wrong, I thought he was a little disappointed when I told him about the job.

"Have you heard of her?" I asked.

"Yes. She stays up here when she's in between movies. I've done some work in her house."

I'd never thought about him doing anything but running the cabins.

"What do you do?"

"I'm a carpenter by trade," he said. "I still do odd jobs for people when they need help."

"That's why you know so many different things," I said.

"Say, I'm cookin' up some stew, why don't you come down and join me and Mabel for dinner a little later."

"That sounds delicious," I said. "What time?"

"Around five?"

"That's perfect. It'll give me a chance to read a little and take a quick nap."

Mabel walked me to my cabin, and I said, "Go on, girl. Go back home now."

As if she understood, she turned and ran back to the office. Once inside, I lit my fireplace to knock the chill off the cabin, then lit another match to the candle lamp. Even in the early afternoon, the ceiling light wasn't bright enough to read by. I brought my book over and then huddled under a heavy quilt. I buried my nose in it—I was freezing, and the sudden sound of wind howling outside only made me colder.

I could feel the tiredness spread across my face and body—and realized I was drained. Two hours later, I woke to a setting sun and a darkening sky. I had no idea what time it was, and I made myself a mental note to ask Mr. Maynard if he had an extra clock I could use.

I splashed water on my face and changed my clothes. I hoped dinner was ready.

The lights were on in the office when I went down, and our meal smelled delicious. I called out to Mr. Maynard.

"In here," he replied.

Mabel came to show me the way.

"It smells wonderful. I should have helped you."

"No, you're our guest tonight, right, girl?"

Silverware was out, so I set the table, and then got us each a glass of water.

"Go ahead and sit. I'll bring everything to the table. There's plenty, so don't be shy."

"This is delicious," I said after taking my first bite.

"I can cook a few things, but not many."

"I don't cook at all. We all ate at the servant's table down in the kitchen, so I'll probably make someone a terrible wife."

"You'll just need to marry a man who either doesn't care, or who can do the cookin' himself." Mr. Maynard chuckled.

I felt my face drain.

"Are you all right?" Mr. Maynard asked.

After what'd I done, and now with a baby due, I was certain I'd never find a man who would marry the likes of me.

"I'm fine," I lied. "Just overly hungry."

While we ate, Mr. Maynard said, "So, Ruth Ann Landry, tell me something about yourself that I already don't know."

I panicked. What did he know about me? Had he talked with Charlotte or Clara when we were up with Miles and Finn? Had he discovered I was pregnant?

"I didn't mean to startle you," he said.

"It's okay." I paused. "Let me think."

Thankfully, Mabel came to me and nudged my hand to either pet her or give her something to eat.

I told him we were originally from Tennessee, and that when my father lost his job at the railway, we came to Seattle.

"My mother found a job working for a family, and when one of the maids was let go, they hired me. Then I came up here with my friends, and that's about it."

I left out all the other details.

"And do you plan on staying up here?"

"I think so. It's very peaceful, and I feel comfortable here." I quickly changed the subject. "And what about you? What brought you up here?"

"Well, I was a carpenter down in Los Angeles, Hollywood actually, and when the movie studio planned to do a film up here, they asked me if I was interested in building cabins that would house the actors. They paid me and then gave me the cabins and the land. It was a deal I couldn't pass up. I'd been seeing someone in Los Angeles, but when it didn't work out, I decided to start over, and I moved up here permanently. I started building and doing repairs, and put a sign out and rented the cabins when someone wanted one.

"I also worked on the dam, and I'm still the only guy who'll go down in the tower elevator to release water when needed. I'll show it to you the next time we go to the Village. And then I'm also a volunteer fireman. We have one fire truck up here, and most of the time, buildings just burn because we can't get to them."

"That's terrible," I said. "I couldn't imagine losing my home to fire."

A shadow crossed his face, and when he looked at me, his face softened. "It's a good place to start over, fall in love and get married. That's if it's what you want to do."

"I haven't found love yet," I murmured.

"You will, Ruth. You have a long life ahead of you. You will."

Mabel broke the silence with a whimper.

"May I feed her a bit?"

"Yes. She's really taken a liking to you."

"As I have to her. I never had a pet before."

"They bring love to your life. Until you have one of your own, you can love Mabel."

I lowered my head.

"Thank you."

CHAPTER FOURTEEN

The fire crackled, and I turned to look at it, instantly mesmerized by the flames. Mr. Maynard was staring into it as well. The golden flames of the fire cast a warm glow on his face, and I saw a gentleness in him I'd not witnessed in a man before; certainly not in either my father or Mr. Fletcher. For his age, Mr. Maynard was handsome in a rugged way. There was something different about him that evening; he'd had his hair cut, and his beard was neatly trimmed. I would have thought when a man lived by himself, he wouldn't be concerned so much with his personal appearance.

He looked back at me, and I quickly lowered my head to avoid his gaze. I hoped he thought the flush in my face was because of the fire's warmth.

"I've noticed you haven't addressed me as anything since I asked you to call me by my name," he said.

I thought for a moment before I answered.

"I've never really addressed many people, especially men, by their given names."

"I guess that makes sense, given you've always been in someone's employ. But please try; when you call me Mr. Maynard, it sounds so formal. And I think we've become friends, haven't we?"

"Yes, we have. I'll try harder." I wanted to change the subject, so I asked, "Can I help clear the dishes?"

"No. Why don't you just keep Mabel company? I can manage myself."

As I petted Mabel, I continued to watch Mr. Maynard—Jack—as he scraped our food onto one plate and set it down for Mabel's dinner. He then set the dishes and silverware in an enamel wash pan and reached for his washing cloth. He hummed an indistinct tune as he scrubbed and cleaned, and then, after Mabel started licking her dish, he washed that too.

I stood then and took a dishtowel and began drying what he'd just set in the strainer. I turned to watch Mabel as she noisily slurped water from her bowl, making a watery mess on the floor near it.

"Thanks for the wonderful dinner, Mr.—Jack." I stammered.

With a big grin, he said, "Thanks. I'm glad you could join us."

The next morning, the wind picked up again, and I was grateful I had a heavy coat. Patrick pulled up in the drive and I ran out to greet him. Like he'd done before, Jack peered out the window and waved. When we got to Miss Hayes' house, a clean uniform was waiting for me in the back hallway, so I put it on. Already it was a little snug, but I figured I'd be able to hide my situation for a while at least. I was hoping when she realized my predicament, she'd let me stay until she had to go back to Hollywood.

I got everything done, and while I was changing out of my uniform, Miss Hayes was waiting for me outside the door.

"I trust your first day went well?" she asked.

"It did. I hope you're satisfied with my work."

"I believe you'll work out fine," she said, then added, "I see I misjudged the size of your dress, but it's all we have."

"It's fine, really. I just need to go on a diet," I said. "I'll see you the day after tomorrow?"

"Patrick will come pick you up," she said.

The next morning, I rushed down to the office, ducking and swatting at something buzzing around me.

"I have bugs!" I cried out. "They started coming after me when I opened my cabin door. They're flying all around, and I just know I'm going to be stung!"

"Let's go see what's goin' on," Jack said. "You stay here, girl," he said to Mabel.

Our footsteps crunched on the gravel as we made our way down to my cabin.

"I see them," Jack said. "They's hornets is all."

"They weren't here yesterday."

"They're pretty quick setting up a nest. I'll go make up something to get rid of them. Stay away, now."

A few minutes later, he came back with a concoction of cider vinegar, sugar, and water in a spray pump. The minute he aimed it toward the nest and began spraying, hornets flew everywhere.

"Go down to the office. Make sure none of them follow you. We don't want any coming inside. And definitely don't let Mabel out."

When Jack yelled, "Ow," I turned to see him swatting a hornet away. When he came back inside, he applied some of the apple cider vinegar to his bites, then made up a paste of baking soda and water, and then spread that onto the spots.

"Don't you need to pull out the stingers?" I asked.

"Only the females can sting you, and their stingers are smooth, so they don't come off when they get you."

"Oh. I guess there's a lot I need to learn if I'm going to stay up here."

The next time Jack and I went to the Village, he bought more muffins from the bakery and I went to the bookshop. The one Agatha Christie book I'd left behind was nowhere to be seen, but I found two of her books that weren't there before and took them up to the counter.

"I wish I would have bought the book I left behind the last time I was in," I said.

I saw Clyde glance up at Jack, and then he said to me, "I'm sure we'll get more. Just keep checking back with me."

"Oh, I will. I plan to find a large bookcase and fill it."

Jack and I left and then we passed the candy store and I couldn't resist. I splurged and bought chocolate covered almonds and a bag of nonpareils.

"I haven't had either of these since I snatched some out of the candy dish at the Fletchers," I confessed.

"How shocking," he said, raising his eyebrows in jest.

Suddenly, I thought of my mother, and how she must be worried sick about me, and my smile faded. I looked at my chocolates, and I lost my appetite.

"What's happened?" Jack asked.

"I just thought about my mother, and I've suddenly become homesick, I think."

He took my hand, and we walked through a pass way to the lake.

I'd forgotten how beautiful the lake was. When I came up with Charlotte and Clara, we only spent a few minutes looking at the water and all the trees. I was still downhearted, but watching the ducks swim to where we stood at the edge of the lake, I suddenly brightened. They were competing for our attention, and I would quickly learn, for food.

"They're hungry," Jack said. "I should have thought to bring some food."

"Maybe the next time we come, we can do that," I said, feeling better.

"I wanted to show you the tower," he said, pointing to a tall blue tower off to our left. "They built it to release water for irrigation down to San Bernardino, but now it's used to control the lake level."

"And you have to go down there, under the water?"

"Not very often, and it's not as bad as it seems. I guess it would be if you had claustrophobia."

"Well, I'd never do it," I said, cringing.

A misty fog started rolling in and in only a few minutes, we could hardly see the tower. Neither of us had brought our jackets, and the air had turned chilly.

"We should get home," Jack said. "It'll probably get worse the later it gets, and I hate driving when it's so hard to see."

The next time we went in to the feed store, Jack bought a duck food mixture they had, and when we returned to the cabins, he set it down outside the office. With his bone handle pocket knife, he sliced the feed bag open, then went inside and brought out a scoop and some small brown paper bags.

"If you'll scoop up the bags, I'll go get the stapler and staple them up. We can keep 'em in the storeroom, and put some in the truck."

When I stood and stretched after filling the bags, I caught a glimpse of Jack, and it wasn't the first time I'd caught him eyeing me. I tried to pull in my stomach, which was now almost impossible to do. He didn't say a word, but I knew for certain he'd figured it out.

I broke the silence between us, saying, "Even though I was careful, I ended up spilling some feed on the ground. Should I worry about picking it up?"

"No," Jack said. "The squirrels and birds will find it quick enough."

Just as we finished, Patrick came to pick me up, and I waved Jack and Mabel goodbye. I sat in the back of the car and released a huge sigh. I had no idea things were going to get worse.

The moment I walked into the house, Miss Hayes greeted me.

"Is there something you'd like to tell me?" A finely arched eyebrow lifted slightly as she looked first at my stomach, then at my face.

"I'm sorry, ma'am," I stammered. "I desperately needed this job, and I knew if I told you, you never would have hired me." My eyes welled with tears, and I couldn't control them.

"Well, if it makes any difference, you're probably right. But you've done a good job for me, and I wouldn't have fired you if I knew sooner. It's definitely none of my business, since you told me you didn't have a husband. But I'm afraid I'm going to bring you bad news. The studio has called me in early, and I'll be going back to Hollywood in a week. They've upped the production of my film."

"What does that mean, exactly?" I asked.

"It means I won't have any work for you until I return."

Comprehension evaded me for a moment, and I tilted my head in question.

"What I'm saying, Ruth, is that for now, I won't need you. But when I return, if you're still up here and need a job, I'll give you a call. I've never been in your situation, but you've done a good job for me, and you'll have had your baby."

"Shall I work today, then?"

"Yes, we'll need to close up the house. Do one last cleaning and cover everything."

At least I'd have one more day of pay!

When I was ready to leave, Miss Hayes was ready with my pay, and she included an extra dollar tip. "I won't need these," she said, handing me a bag of apples. "Eat them or feed the deer."

"Thank you so much for giving me a chance," I said, wiping more tears from my eyes. "I'm sorry."

"I wish you the best, and I'll be back. Patrick is outside waiting for you, so go with him."

The moment I climbed in to the car, I burst into a new round of tears, and Patrick turned to look at me.

"Are you all right?" he asked.

Of course, I wasn't all right. I'd just lost my job, my pregnancy was out in the open, both with Miss Hayes and with Jack, and I didn't know what I was going to do. I told Patrick as much and he scrunched his mouth in thought.

"I have an idea," he said.

I looked up at him, and suddenly I was choking from my runny nose.

"Here's a napkin," he said, handing me a handful. "I know somewhere that always needs help. You won't be in the public eye, so they probably won't care if you're pregnant. It's not far from here."

By the time I finished blowing my nose, we were turning down a narrow dirt road that led into a forest of tall pine trees. Piles of leaves clustered around brown and orange leafed trees, signifying we were deep into fall. I was glad I'd brought my coat, for suddenly a chill filled the air.

"Here it is," Patrick said as he pulled to the back of a white building with brown wood trim around the windows. "Wait in the car."

I blew my nose once more and tried to think about what I was going to tell Jack. I still had plenty of money to see me through until I had the baby, but that wasn't the problem. The problem was that I had to face Jack, and I worried he wouldn't let me continue to stay in the cabin.

About ten minutes later, Patrick came back to the car, and he had a smile on his face.

"Come with me," he said. "They'll take you on."

"What is this place?" I finally asked.

"It's kind of a hotel. Rich people come here to gamble and sometimes stay. You'll be one of the maids cleaning up the rooms."

"Do I need to interview with anyone?"

"Come with me," Patrick said again.

We entered through the back door and passed a food storeroom and kitchen, then turned down a hallway leading to an office. There I was introduced to a woman named Rita, who was in charge of housekeeping.

"When's the baby due?" she asked.

"In about three months," I said. I hadn't seen a doctor yet, and now that it was going to be public knowledge, I knew I couldn't put it off any longer.

"Well, we need someone to clean the guest rooms, so if you do a good job, and mind your own business, you can stay as long as you're able to work."

"And after the baby? Would you have work for me then?"

"Yes, again, depending on how good a worker you are."

"How many days a week would you need me?"

"Every day. Six or seven days a week, and we pay three dollars a day. Do you have transportation?"

I hadn't thought about getting to and from a job so far from my cabin.

"I can tell by your face you don't. You can stay here for five dollars a month."

I looked at Patrick, who only shrugged.

"I'll take it. When do I start?"

"You can move in tomorrow and start in the afternoon."

"I'll see you then," I said, and motioned for Patrick. It was time for us to leave. I had packing to do, and I had no time to waste.

"Could I ask if you'd take me in tomorrow?"

"I drive Miss Hayes down tomorrow around noon, so I don't see why I can't do it in the morning."

"Thanks, Patrick. I don't know how I'll ever thank you."

I gave him a quick hug.

CHAPTER FIFTEEN

I was so excited to tell Jack about my day, I didn't think anything of him standing there outside the office, Mabel at his side. He had a look about him—like he'd just had the most awful news.

"I've been worried sick about you," he said tersely.

"What bee's got in your bonnet?" I asked, clearly annoyed.

"It's almost dark, and I expected you home over an hour ago."

I was so surprised by his comment; I felt like I was being interrogated and I immediately went on the defensive.

"Well, if it's any of your business, I lost my job today, because, as you've most likely guessed, I'm pregnant. I've seen you look at me," I said defensively. "Well, actually I didn't lose it because of that; Miss Hayes has been called back to Hollywood early, and she doesn't need me."

Jack's face fell.

"And when I told Patrick, he gladly took me to a hotel that needed help!"

I was now angry, and I glared at him. He instantly backed off.

"Where did he take you?" he asked in a calmer voice.

I realized I hadn't asked the name of the hotel, so I told him where it was.

"It's down a narrow dirt road, and the building is white with brown trim."

"Good God, Ruth. That's the Tudor House. It's a speakeasy and a brothel!" Jack threw his hands up in the air and Mabel barked. They were both against me.

I was glad the early evening darkness hid the burning in my cheeks. I was both humiliated and annoyed at the same time, and I was aware of Jack's scrutiny. He must have thought I was the dumbest person alive!

I stomped away towards my cabin, and as I fumbled with my keys, I began to cry again. It seemed that lately, crying had become my coping mechanism, and I was angry with myself for being so sensitive.

Jack had followed me to my cabin.

"Ruth," he said kindly, touching my arm. "I shouldn't have acted that way, but I was worried. Can we at least talk?"

I suddenly had a terrible headache, no doubt from my on and off bouts of tears, and I rubbed my temples.

"Come in," I said. "I'll start a fire."

I unlocked the door and Mabel literally galloped in, stopping first at my bed to inspect it, then jumping on it. She turned in circles before she found a comfortable spot and laid down.

Jack put some new logs on the grate, and I added some kindling and pine needles for the fragrance. He started the fire, and within a few minutes, it was crackling and popping. I lit the lamp and set it on the table between the two chairs facing the fireplace.

"Did them boys do that to you?" he finally asked.

It took me a moment to figure out who he was talking about.

"No," I said, tears welling up again in my eyes.

"Aw, Ruthie, please don't cry," Jack said, coming to sit on the floor in front of me. He took both my hands in his.

All at once, I let it out.

"I knew for sure I was pregnant when I took the job at the hotel. I'd come to Los Angeles with the family I worked for, and when Mr. Fletcher came to my room while his family was downstairs eating dinner, I knew it had to stop. I told him so." I started crying again and wiped my tears. After a long and exhausted sigh, I continued. "And then Charlotte said

I could go with her and her friends up to the mountains. It was a way for me to escape."

Jack tilted his head back and closed his eyes. The fire had warmed up the cabin and I could hear Mabel snoring on my bed.

"I left my mother, who must be worried sick about me, and I can't write her, or the family will know where I am. When Miss Hayes said my job with her was finished, I knew where Patrick took me wasn't the best place, but I needed a way to support myself and my baby when it comes."

Jack pulled me up out of my chair and held me.

"Ruth, I love you."

I started to pull away from him, but he held me firmly.

"I think I knew it the minute you came back up here. I also figured you were coming up here to get away from something, just like I'd done. If you'll have me, I want you to be my wife. I'll take care of the baby, and if you want, we can have some of our own."

He let me step back from him, now, and I could see the tenderness in his eyes. Jack Maynard was a handsome man, and while I hadn't started out thinking I could marry someone like him, I now could envision a life with him. I didn't love him in the romantic sense of the word; other than Mr. Fletcher, and any romantic notions I'd had about *him*, I hadn't ever experienced passion. I wondered if by being with Jack, with someone as caring as he was, if I could learn to love him that way.

As if it was a test on my part, Jack stayed with me in my cabin that night. Once we had Mabel on her own blanket by the fire, we stood and held each other as if we were dancing. He kissed my forehead, then my lips. When he started to slip my dress off, at first I froze, for I'd never bared myself, even to Mr. Fletcher. Jack sensed my hesitation, and gently ran his fingers over my shoulders and down my arms, sending a tingling sensation throughout my body. When my dress finally fell to the floor, he watched me intently as his hands made their way down my body, touching my rounded belly, and cupping it in his hands. His gentle caresses told me in no uncertain terms, he would love me, and my baby.

His eagerness excited me, and soon I welcomed him in. Afterwards, I could hear his breathing as he slept, and I watched him in the fire's light. When he woke, he reached for me and touched my stomach first.

"I haven't hurt him, have I?"

"I don't think so. I think he knows how you've made me feel."

We lay there in the comfort of each other's arms, and then I asked, "What will people say when we tell them we're married?"

"I don't give a damn what they say if you want to know the truth. They'll love you as much as I do, and if they don't, it doesn't matter."

The next morning, after Jack left for a job, I dressed for a warm day and took Mabel with me on a walk. We climbed down an embankment where I'd heard a creek run, and I realized I actually liked the smells of the forest—leaves, logs, moss and pine. Clusters of small trees, which I'd later learn were called saplings, were randomly scattered around the enormous trees that had been there for years.

Mabel barked and ran to the sound of rustling in the bushes to our right. A small red fox poked its head out to see what we were doing, and Mabel barked again and quivered with excitement.

"Stay," I called, although I did not know if she even knew what the command meant.

Surprisingly she did, but she whined. "Stay," I said again.

Out of nowhere, a second fox poked its head out, then they both just as quickly backed in to the bush and scampered away. We walked a little farther until we came to the stream, and Mabel stopped to take a drink.

I'd smelled the scent of rain on asphalt before, but I'd never smelled it in the air like I did up here. Without notice, the skies opened up, and within moments, Mabel and I were drenched. I turned my face skyward and let the rain wet my face. Mabel shook herself, and then ran up the embankment, all the while turning back to bark at me. "Let's go home," she seemed to say.

CHAPTER SIXTEEN

The next week, for my eighteen birthday, Jack took me down to San Bernardino to the J. C. Penney's store where we picked out our wedding rings. He knew he wanted a simple band, and after looking at all the different options in the jewelry case, I decided on a band also. We had them both inscribed with our initials.

We'd found a crib and dresser at the second-hand store in town, but I needed a mattress, sheets, a few newborn things and diapers, so we went to the baby department next. I could feel myself glowing when the sales clerk asked when our baby was due, especially when I saw Jack winking at me.

There were no shops in the mountains that had the kind of wedding dress I needed; one that would do a good job covering my condition, so we went to the dress department, where several dress styles were on display with a discreet sign that read, "Designer clothing with concealed tucks to allow for necessary expansion." They were priced at almost thirteen dollars, which was exorbitant in my opinion, but Jack insisted I buy one.

"It's a special occasion," he said.

By the time we were finished, I was exhausted and my feet and ankles had swollen.

"What say we stop at the soda fountain and splurge?" Jack suggested.

Suddenly, something decadent sounded wonderful, and we carried all our purchases downstairs.

Three weeks later, we stood in front of the justice of the peace down in San Bernardino, and a couple that was getting married after us stood up as our witnesses. When it was Jack's turn to say "I do", I saw something in his eyes that made my pulse quicken. It was impossible not to return his suggestive smile.

It was November, 1930, and it was the happiest day of my life.

Even though my marriage to Jack Maynard wasn't what I would have called a conventional one, I wanted to wait until after we were married to move my things into the office. Our bedroom was on the smallish size, but perfect for two people. We set the crib and extra dresser up on one wall for when the baby came. Jack said he'd add on another bedroom after winter.

Because I was embarrassed, I'd put off having a pregnancy exam, but now that I was married, I went to see the town doctor. His initial reaction to seeing me in my condition was professional, but the surprise in his eyes gave him away.

"I'm glad you came in," he finally said after examining me. "Everything looks fine, and I suspect you'll be a mother in about a month."

There was a small hospital in town, and he told me when I was ready, to call him and head there. Once it became known we were married, a few of the local women stopped by and brought baby clothing their children had outgrown; we had coffee and cookies, and they offered to be of help any time I needed anything.

"Emma couldn't make it by," one of them said, and I caught her looking at the other women.

"I'm eternally grateful," I said to them all as they left, relieved they all received me the way they did.

We had our first snow in December and I remember waking to a blanket of white covering tree branches and the land around the cabins. I looked out our bedroom window and caught a glimpse of a squirrel as it quickly scampered across the ground and up a tree. I would try to remember to set out some nuts.

I went to the front door and even though the air was cold, it smelled fresh and clean. I was surprised how quiet everything was. Suddenly Jack was behind me, wiping the sleep from his eyes, and he said, "You'll catch your death standing there in the cold. Close the door and I'll relight the fire."

I could tell I was getting close to my time. My lower back had started aching, and sometimes no matter how hard I tried to get comfortable, I couldn't get the pain to stop radiating down my legs. It came and went, along with the feeling I was in my monthlies. I had an appointment to see my doctor in a few days, and I would ask him then when he thought I'd start labor.

Jack treated me like a queen. He didn't want me to do anything but sit, which, of course, made me feel like an invalid. Mabel kept me company when I sat and read, and she'd lay her head on my legs and look up at me. When she'd whine, I'd tell her I was doing all right, and she'd go back to sleep.

I'd never had my own Christmas tree, so Jack cut one from the property and he made a two-by-four stand for the trunk. I found an old plaid blanket and laid it on the floor, and wrapped it around the base of the tree. I made Jack take me in to the second-hand store in town, and I bought some tinsel, hand-blown glass ornaments and a tree topper. It wasn't much; not at all like the tall trees that used to decorate the grand entry hall at the mansion, but it was ours, and it was a beginning.

"Come with me," Jack said. "I want to show you something."

I followed him outside, and behind the cabins was a clump of birch trees with random clusters of green leaves growing on otherwise bare branches.

"This is mistletoe."

I watched as he carefully cut some stems, and he handed them to me.

"It's actually a parasite. Birds carry it from tree to tree."

He could tell by the look on my face, I hadn't comprehended what he was telling me, so he continued.

"Birds eat the berries, poop out the seeds onto branches, and mistletoe grows."

"*How lovely,*" I said in jest. "That takes the Christmas spirit out of things."

We brought several bunches in and I tied red ribbon around the stems, and we hung them from the doorways in the office.

We'd agreed we wouldn't buy any presents this year, knowing we'd spent a lot on getting ready for our wedding and buying baby things. But when Christmas morning arrived, Jack gave me the Agatha Christie book he'd bought at the bookshop the day I'd had to choose between three books. And I gave him a silver belt buckle he could wear on special occasions.

CHAPTER SEVENTEEN

On January 1, 1931, I gave birth to a beautiful baby girl, and we named her Dorothy after my mother, and Rose after Jack's mother. The Mountain News came and took her picture in the hospital being the first baby born in the mountains in the New Year. When I saw us on the front page, I was so proud of my new family. That was until I realized anyone who read the paper would know where I was! Jack tried to reason with me that someone in Seattle wasn't likely to read a small town paper from Lake Arrowhead.

"I think you need to contact your mother, anyway," Jack said.

"I can't. The family will know she's received a letter and then she'll get in trouble. It doesn't mean I don't miss her terribly," I said.

And I did. I'd thought about her toiling for that family every day, wishing I could talk to her about what had happened, but mostly wanting her to know I was all right. She'd wanted to make a better world for me, and I knew it was challenging for her to stay with my father. She taught me to read and write, and gave me the love of books. She was patient but strong, and when I had baby Dorothy, I understood how much she loved me.

I would write to her one day, just not right now.

In the spring, Jack taught me how to drive his truck. First, he had me practice shifting the gears while we were parked on our land, and then, while he held Dorothy, I managed to get us out onto the road. The truck jerked and stuttered, and I killed the engine while learning to coordinate my hands and feet. At one point, I was laughing so hard, I had to pull over; I couldn't see for the tears in my eyes. And looking at terror-struck Jack made me laugh even harder.

I didn't give up, and neither did he, and eventually I could tie Dorothy to the seat and drive anywhere.

Once a week, we'd make the trip into town, frequenting our favorite stores. I always bought a book from Clyde in the village and then we bought a few pieces of chocolate candy and muffins for our guests. We brought duck food, and baby Dorothy delighted in seeing the ducks come to greet us. She watched as we tossed food into the air and I knew by the way she lifted her little arms, she wanted to do it too.

We got our first Sears catalog in the mail, and when it came, I pored over it for hours, reading every advertisement whether it was for something I needed or not. I found some work clothes for me: pants, boots and sensible shirts that would make my chores—gardening, clearing leaves and cleaning the cabins—easier. I'll never forget the first time I wore my new work clothes into town; some men and women looked at me disapprovingly, but I took their foolishness with a grain of salt.

Around a week later, Mrs. Jessop from the post office asked me where I got my work boots.

"Out of the Sears catalog," I answered.

She checked to make sure no one was within listening distance, then asked, "And them pants?"

Soon, several women came to town in their work clothes, and whenever they saw me walking by, they nodded whether or not they knew me.

That summer, Jack bought us a new Zenith radio. Our old one was small, and the speakers crackled so badly, we couldn't always hear what the characters were saying. I loved the *Jack Benny Show*, and Jack favored *The Shadow* and *The Green Hornet*. But *Amos 'n' Andy* was his favorite, and for the longest time, we assumed the two characters were Negroes; I thought it was wonderful they had such popular jobs. I'd only seen one Negro family up there at that time; Abe and Athena. He worked with the blacksmith caring for the horses, trimming and shoeing their hooves, and Athena was a house maid like I had been. One day, Jack read a newspaper article revealing the real story about Amos and Andy; they were white!

During the day, I always tried to find time to listen to my favorite soap operas—so named because Lever Brothers and other soap manufacturers often sponsored them. I knew they were trying to appeal to women, and they did a good job. Sometimes I'd overhear women in the post office talk about the latest program. For a long time, I didn't tell Jack I listened to them, fearing he'd think I was silly. But one day I left the tuner knob at my channel, and that night when Jack turned the radio on, there was only static. He scratched his beard in thought and changed the channel.

"Now I know what you do all day," he said then, clearly amused.

As the days grew warmer, I took baby Dorothy out and I'd spread a blanket and sit under one of our pine trees, watching her discover so many new things, including her feet. I'd bring one of my books out and read. I never tired of fresh air and the smell of pine. Sometimes, if Jack was home, he'd sit with me and we'd have sandwiches and tea. I'd read while he and Dorothy napped. Many times I'd think about my mother and my old life, and each time I did, I couldn't deny how fulfilling my life was now.

We didn't have a lot of guests that summer, and I worried we'd run low on money. But Jack stayed busy building the new library in town, and he brought his pay home every week. I thought about asking if I could get a part-time job there since I loved books so much, and when Jack said he thought it was a great idea, I put my name in the hat. Not long after that, they sent me a letter telling me I could have a job there, and I was in seventh heaven. On the days I worked, I'd be surrounded by the things I loved most: books.

Toward the fall, I recognized the signs of morning sickness, but waited a few weeks to tell Jack he was going to be a father again. I'd heard of women losing their babies early, and I didn't want to disappoint him. A year ago, I'd had terrible thoughts about the baby I was carrying, but now, I couldn't even imagine losing a child.

When I told him, he was crazy with happiness. He danced me around the office, and baby Dorothy laughed. I knew he'd want a boy, and I prayed that's what we'd have.

"I'll have to build two bedrooms now," he said. "I'll have them finished in plenty of time."

I decided then it was time I wrote to my mother.

I told her how I'd been afraid to contact her, for fear the family would retaliate against her. I knew she would have been worried sick when they returned from their trip and I was nowhere to be found. And I prayed images of me lying dead somewhere hadn't consumed her.

I told her I'd left because of Mr. Fletcher and that I had been pregnant. For a long time, I worried about what I was going to do, and there was no way I'd be able to return home and face the shame. Of course I'd have been blamed, and I never could have told anyone the truth.

I told her about baby Dorothy, named after her, and how beautiful a child she was. And that I'd married Jack Maynard, who took me in when I needed a place to stay.

"He is a wonderful man, and a good father." I wrote. "And we're going to have a second child."

I told her my life in the mountains was fulfilling and that I was happy.

"Would you want us to visit?" I asked. "When the family sees I've written, it'll be the worst for you. Would you lose your job? We have seven cabins that Jack built for the movie studio, and we rent them out. Would you consider moving away from Seattle? There is plenty of room for you here."

I signed it, "Your daughter Ruth Ann."

A week later, while on our trip into town, a letter from my mother was sitting in our post office box. I'd waited in the truck as baby Dorothy was sleeping, and I had such mixed emotions when Jack brought it out to me. I was almost sick to my stomach wondering if she was going to be angry with me and her letter would tell me she never wanted to speak to me again. Or she could say she forgave me for taking so long to let her know I was alive and well.

Unable to gather the courage to read it, I set it in my purse.

"Aren't you going to read it?" Jack asked.

"I can't. I'm too nervous."

About ten minutes later, I stopped fidgeting and tore open the envelope.

"My dearest daughter,

When the Fletchers returned without you, all I could think about was the last time I saw you...had I told you to return safely? Why would I have? There are no words to describe how I felt. I struggled with my everyday chores along with those they added, and Mrs. Fletcher even called me in to remind me I had my work to do. You would have thought as a mother, she would have understood my grief. I think she was angry you'd left.

At night, I cried myself to sleep, and every morning I prayed I'd hear from you and that you'd return.

And now, my prayers have been answered, and I thank God you're alive. You have no idea how many times I imagined you in danger, and I'm just so thankful you're okay.

And I have a granddaughter! How beautiful she must be.

I'm certain the Fletchers know I've received a letter from you; nothing escapes them, and I have no idea how they will treat me from now on. Part of me hopes they will still welcome me here, but the other part says they deserve to know the truth.

I haven't thought it all the way through yet. I wanted first to send this to let you know I'd received your letter.

With all my love, Mother"

CHAPTER EIGHTEEN

Jack Maynard Jr. was born in June 1932, and as promised, Jack had the new bedrooms finished. He extended the pine flooring and log walls so that it didn't look like an addition, and I found a large rug and another dresser the last time we'd gone into town. Baby Jack was a crier, and he kept us both up at night no matter how we coddled him. He developed red splotches on his cheeks that the doctor called eczema. We had to constantly clean his face, and we only used Ivory soap for our laundry. The grocer brought it in especially for us, so we wouldn't have to go down the mountain for it. It was months before his skin cleared up, and when we went into town, I could tell by the way people looked at him, they thought I wasn't taking good enough care of him.

In August, Jack came to me and told me we'd need to put Mabel down. We'd talked about how she was having a hard time getting around and while she tried her best to keep up with us, her back legs just didn't want to cooperate. I couldn't bear to go with him when he took her to the shelter, and for that, I felt like a coward.

When he returned with her leash, I cried with him, understanding we'd lost our best friend.

A week later, at the grocer's, we saw a notice on the bulletin board advertising free puppies. Jack wanted to go down to the new shelter in San Bernardino and rescue a dog that was certain to be put to sleep if it didn't find a home.

There were so many to choose from, at first it was overwhelming. There were all different sizes and breeds, barking and coming up to the cage as we walked past; I read their minds, as they pleaded, "pick me."

Jack kept returning to one mixed breed puppy that licked his face when he bent down to pet it.

"This is the one," he said. "She looks a little like Mabel, and she loves to kiss."

We called her Mabeltwo.

At the beginning of fall, we drove up to Seattle to bring my mother back down. I'd forgotten how large the city was, and it had grown even more since I'd been gone. We had a map with us, but more than once, I asked Jack to pull in to a filling station so I could ask directions. When we got to a point where I finally recognized my surroundings, I relaxed.

As we drove up to the mansion, Jack whistled at its grandeur.

"It sure is something," he said.

"Yes, it is," I said. "But the only good people inside are the servants."

I'd wrestled with the idea of confronting Mr. Fletcher if I saw him, but when I told Jack about my thoughts, he told me that doing so wasn't going to change anything, and that I'd be better off if I kept my thoughts to myself. Of course, that made me want to do it even more. I was glad I had a few days on the drive up there to think about it more. In the end, I decided to leave it at only saying hello to Cook and the laundress if they could sneak out the back door.

"My goodness," Cook said, enveloping me in a big hug. "Look at you. All grown up, and a mother at that!"

Her smile faded a little, and she grew serious as she took a better look at Dorothy. Her eyebrow rose slightly as she turned to me.

"I named her after my mother," I said quickly. "And this is baby Jack Jr., named after his daddy."

"Well, they sure are handsome children. And lucky," she said, holding Jack's little hand.

"I'm the one who's lucky. I have what I never thought I'd be able to have. A family," I said, glancing at Jack as he helped my mother put her things in the back of the truck.

"Mr. Fletcher said to give you this," Cook said, handing me an envelope.

He'd addressed it to me, and my first thought was to hand it right back to her. But by the feel, I could tell something was folded inside, and curiosity got the better of me. I tucked it into my purse and then gave Cook a big hug.

She handed me a heavy sack, and even before I opened it, I could smell her fresh bread. When I looked inside, there was cheese and a jar of her wonderful preserves.

"I've missed you," I said. "And I'll never forget you spoiling me with treats from the kitchen, knowing full well you could be caught and reprimanded. Like now."

"Oh pfft," she said. "We've missed you too, Ruthie. But it looks like you've made a good life for yourself. No one can begrudge you for that."

"I don't have much," my mother said, handing Jack her last suitcase.

He tied it into the bed of the truck, then he said, "It's going to be a tight fit inside, but we'll make it."

I gave Cook one last hug and then, for some reason, looked up at the windows to see if anyone was watching us from upstairs. I'd have been lying if I said I was a little disappointed no one was there. I let my breath out, and then out of the corner of my eye, I was certain I saw a curtain moving. Whoever was there was gone before I had a chance to glimpse them.

My mother and I each took a child to sit on our lap, and after a deep sigh from both of us, we began our return trip to the mountains. To save money, we all slept in one room when we stopped for the night; the children between Jack and me in one bed, and my mother in another. Indeed, it was a long trip back home. But once we turned onto Highway 18 and started to climb the hill, I, for one, sighed in relief. We were almost home.

I'd forgotten the envelope in my purse until I needed a tissue, and as my hand brushed against it, I hoped the alarm I felt didn't show on my face. I quickly blew my nose, closed my purse and set it on the floorboard behind my feet.

Once I got my mother settled into her cabin, I bathed the children and put them to bed. While Jack got Mabeltwo from our neighbor, I took my purse and went into the bathroom. I quickly opened the envelope and counted the hundred dollars Mr. Fletcher had tucked inside. There was no note.

Mother spent the first week of her new life up here getting to know Dorothy and Jack Jr., and learning about mountain life. She loved walking the property with me and the children, and it seemed almost every day she would make some comment on how beautiful it was up here. I could tell she felt the same sense of delight as I did when she heard the pine needles and dried leaves crunch underfoot.

"Do you smell the pine?" I asked.

"The mountains calm me," she said one day. "And I love all the colors."

She saw her first Steller's Jays with their spiked feather tops, when she looked up to see them clustered in a tree, chattering like a group of old friends. And she loved watching the birds land and eat from the feeders.

"Can I fill their feeders?" she asked.

She helped me with my chores and instead of paying rent for her cabin, she offered to clean them when guests left, which seemed fair enough to me and Jack. We took her into town so she could see the Village and feed the ducks. I showed her the bookshop, and I bought a new book, and then we bought muffins at the bakery for the guests due in.

Jack shot his first deer that year, and we took it to the grocer who butchered it for us. We had plenty of meat, so we shared some of it with the neighbor who'd watched Mabeltwo while we were gone. The rest went down into the ice house. Jack had always wanted a deer head on the fireplace, so we took the head to a man who could mount it. Once it was up on the wall, for the longest time, I had a hard time looking that deer in the eyes, thinking he was watching me, blaming me for allowing him to be hung up there. But I eventually got used to it.

My mother had saved her wages, and I thought now that she was here, she should quit working. But she said she wouldn't know what to do with herself if she did. I told her there was work up here, if that's what she wanted. For a few weeks, she read the newspaper, hoping something promising would be posted, and just when she was losing hope, she saw the ad for a housekeeper at the resort. She quickly called and spoke with the manager, who asked her to come in for an interview. The next morning, I dropped Jack off at his job and drove Mother to the Village.

I took the children to feed the ducks, and after about thirty minutes, I began to worry about the interview. Maybe she'd be competing with a lot of younger women and would be passed over. We parked back near the entrance of the hotel and impatiently waited for her to come out. And then I saw her walking toward us, with a grin on her face, and she held some papers up in the air.

"I got the job," she said. "I can start in the morning if you'll give me a ride."

She chatted all the way home, telling me how large the resort was, how the manager introduced her to the head housekeeper, who was surprisingly welcoming and not resentful of her many years of experience.

"They told me they were tired of hiring young girls who only stayed until they could find someone to marry, and that they wanted someone more mature, who would value her job."

She brought little Dorothy to her lap and hugged her.

"They even have housing for their workers..." she said.

I turned and looked at her, surprised she'd even consider such a thing.

"I hope you told them you had a place to stay?"

"I did. But if I ever become a burden to you, Ruthie, I can always stay there. I just want you to know."

"We'll be fine. I want you to see your grandchildren. And Jack and I will make sure you get to work on time."

"Okay, if you're sure," she said, then kissed little Dorothy's cheek.

For the first two weeks, Jack made sure I had access to the truck, but when he finished the job he was on and got a new one in the opposite direction of the Village, I could tell he was growing concerned with the conflicting work schedules. Sometimes he had to go pick up supplies, and if he dropped my mother off first, he worried he'd run late and get behind.

One of the many wonderful qualities about Jack was that he never showed any anxiety in front of my mother. He never made her feel unwelcome, or in the way. So one day, when I showed him the newspaper, I told him I had a solution to our problem.

"There's a car here for sale, and it's two hundred dollars. I've saved a hundred dollars, and I'm sure Mother has some money she could pitch in. I could drive her to work, and we'd have a car large enough for the whole family if we wanted to go out."

Jack scratched his head and thought for a minute, then said, "Well, we could go look at it. Talk to your mother first."

I did, and she thought it was a great idea. The next day, we had a 1929 Ford woody station wagon.

CHAPTER NINETEEN

I hadn't decided what I was going to give my mother for Christmas that year, and with only a few days to spare, I stumbled upon a lovely silver locket that would be perfect for her. I was at the secondhand store, looking for little things I could put in the children's stockings, and I couldn't believe my luck. The minute I got home, I found photos of the children and cut them down to fit each frame. Then I dug around in my gift wrapping drawer and chose a small box that didn't look too worn, wrapped it up and tucked it inside a knitted stocking I'd bought at the same time. I hung it alongside the children's stockings on the fireplace mantel.

Jack desperately needed a heavy winter jacket, so I splurged and ordered him one from the Sears catalog. Thankfully, it came when he wasn't home, and I was able to wrap it in a box and hide it in Dorothy's closet.

Because I saw him measuring and building it, it was impossible for him to keep it a secret, but Jack built me a pine bookcase that fit perfectly on one wall in the office. My book collection had been growing and even *I* was growing tired of stacks of books lying around on the floor. Plus, Dorothy had discovered them and constantly delighted in knocking them over. I organized them alphabetically by author and set those I hadn't read on one end. I still had room to decorate the shelves with pinecones, bookends, and knick knacks I'd found at the secondhand store.

We managed to hide the toy chest Jack built for Dorothy, and on Christmas morning, I tied a large red bow on it and it was waiting for her when she got up. It was perfect for the toys she played with every day, and when we knew we had guests coming up, I'd quickly tuck everything away so we didn't look like a nursery. Mother also got a handmade chest to keep at the end of her bed, where she could store extra winter blankets.

Always the practical one, Jack got me a knitted beanie hat and gloves to match, and *The Great Gatsby*.

Mother and I had gone to the grocers, and we must have spent an hour filling up two boxes of supplies to make Christmas dinner. With her help, I cooked my first turkey. I'd seen Cook do it a hundred times, but I was still nervous as all get out. We made mashed potatoes, gravy, green beans, succotash, and biscuits. We also made a pie with the apples from our tree, and after dinner, we listened to a music program on the radio.

There was always something about the economic downturn in the paper, and every week I read about someone committing suicide, losing his job, going hungry and becoming homeless or getting evicted from their homes. Most people up here didn't have the money to invest in the stock market, so no one we knew lost any money in the crash of '29, but we'd seen a slowdown in the cabin rentals in the year I'd been up there. Jack said not as many people were coming up to vacation so we took a dollar off if someone stayed two nights. I couldn't really say that brought more people up, but it made us feel we were doing our part to help the economy.

In the summer of 1933, the town celebrated the grand opening of the new library. They'd ordered all new books which of course were in bookcases inside, and they filled the parking lot with tables of their old books. People came from all over the mountain to see it and there was even a contest to see who brought back the oldest overdue book. I brought Dorothy and Jack inside and we sat and listened while a librarian read to us from the children's section, then I went outside and looked for books I hadn't read. I ended up with a box full of them, and Jack looked at me sideways, as if asking where I planned to put them all. Poor Clyde; I was certain his book sales came to a screeching halt that weekend.

On the Friday before the July Fourth weekend, the mountain came alive. Overheated cars lined the highway, from pulling their wooden Chris-Craft boats and camping trailers. They were coming for the boat parade and fireworks, and like the rest of our holiday weekends, the town's population swelled by several thousand people. All our cabins were spoken for, which was a welcome relief.

Jack loved watching the boats tour round and round the lake, with their American flags fluttering in the wind at the stern of each boat. I had to admit the sound of their roaring engines vibrated in my chest, and I understood his fascination with them.

"I have a chance to work on one next weekend," Jack said. "The owner's going to leave it up here."

His carpentry business kept him pretty busy, but he somehow found time to work on a few boats, especially if they were stored up here. He wanted to go to the lake so he could show me this boat he was so excited about, so I bundled baby Jack up, and even though it was a warm day, I made sure little Dorothy had a sweater. I'd brought duck food so she could toss some through the open iron railing.

"Be careful," I reminded her.

"That's the one," Jack said, pointing to the boat as it passed us.

I was disappointed he wouldn't have the next weekend to spend with the family, but we could use the money.

"If you want to take the truck back, I'll hang out here," he said, knowing I wouldn't be able to keep Dorothy occupied for much longer, and I was still nursing Jack. Plus, we had another guest checking in after lunch.

"We should have picked up muffins," he said.

"I'll get them," I said, thinking I could make a quick trip to the bookshop and pick up a book I had on layaway. Even though it was early when we returned home, I gave the children their baths. I knew by the time we got back home from watching the fireworks that night, it would be past their bedtime. Just before dark, I packed the children and my mother up, and somehow found a space in the full parking lot at the Village. I made my way through the crowd of people milling around and miraculously found Jack, talking with some men. When he saw me, he broke away, and said, "I saved us a table in front of the Waffle House. I promised them I'd order us sodas."

I handed him baby Jack in the handled basket I carried him in and I unpacked the sandwiches I'd made. It soon grew dark enough to start the fireworks. The sky filled with crackling and popping, in red, white, and blue bursts of color. Baby Dorothy was mesmerized by them, and little Jack slept through it all.

"Pop," she said, pointing to the sky.

"Yes, pop," Jack said.

The wooden boats circled the lake, honking their horns, and we waved at them although they couldn't really see us.

That night, as we lay in bed, we heard smatterings of fireworks go off, and I knew Jack was worried about the recklessness of some people and the possibility of a forest fire. The random gun shots worried us both.

On Sunday, the town held its annual country fair, and people crowded in to see all the booths. There were cookies, hot dogs, bar-b-que, bags of popcorn, and all kinds of pies and cakes. One area was devoted to rabbits, ducks, chickens, turkeys and even reptiles. Jack vied for stuffed animals pitching baseballs at beer bottles, throwing darts at balloons and shooting water guns. Eventually, he won a teddy bear for Dorothy, who, by this time, was starting to cry in frustration.

When the fiddlers started playing, we watched dancers stomp their feet in the dirt, but by then, my mother, the children and I were fading and we needed to get back and check out our guests. While Jack made sure that was done, I put the children down and took a nap.

With two young ones, Jack didn't want me to work. In a way, I agreed with him. I'd have to pay someone to watch them, and when I figured it out, I'd be working for half the money I used to make. I constantly tried to think of ways to save money. Jack helped me till a little plot of land, and I planted a small garden; mainly carrots, tomatoes, beans and cucumbers. I tried canning some of it, but I hated the process, so a neighbor and I traded; I gave her my extras and she canned her strawberries, grapes and peaches for me.

We'd also planted two apple trees the year before, but by the time they bore fruit, the deer had eaten everything on the low-lying branches, and Jack had to climb on a ladder to pick what was left. He'd always leave a few laying on the ground, especially if the birds had gotten to them. So much for not feeding the wildlife!

I was never a great cook, but I learned to save all our leftovers and make them into stews, pot pies, and meatloaf. Mabeltwo still got whatever I couldn't figure out what to do with.

At the end of summer, while at the grocers, I saw a notice on the bulletin board for a used sewing machine. I'd never sewn anything before, but I could see the value of learning. We bought most of our clothing from the second-hand store, or neighbors dropped clothing by for the children. I called the number on the ad, and an older woman answered.

"I'm calling about the sewing machine?" I said.

"Why, yes, dear. I still have it. Do you want to come see it?" she asked.

"Yes. I haven't sewn before, though."

"Well, it sounds like you're young enough to learn."

The next morning, I packed the children up and, after dropping Jack off at a job site, I drove the truck to the address she'd given me. When I pulled up, I saw an old faded truck with a rusted and dented fender sitting there in grass almost a foot high. The rest of the yard was filled with old discarded tires, a car battery, a wooden dog house that looked ready to collapse, a rusty bed frame, a wheelbarrow and some old farm implements. That was something I'd noticed about some people up here who had land; there were no rules about keeping your yard clean, and they just kept collecting their junk.

The front door was open, and I could tell the screen door needed re-screening, and when I knocked a woman said, "C'mon in."

"I'm here about the sewing machine?" I called out. I turned to check the children in the truck before I went in.

The interior of the house was surprisingly clean. The furniture was old and worn, but when I got a glimpse of the kitchen, there wasn't a sink full of dirty dishes. An old dog and cat lay curled together at the woman's feet.

When the dog lifted its head, the woman said, "Don't mind Harriet. She's so old she couldn't protect me or bite you if she wanted to. And the cat's not much better. Hmph."

I saw the sewing machine to my left, and even from a distance, I could tell it was in pretty good shape.

"I haven't sewed in forever," the woman said. "It's a shame to just let it sit here. If it was up to my husband, it'd be outside with all his junk." She hmphed again. "If I can get up, I'll show you how the darned thing works."

It took her two tries before she could get out of the chair, and I watched her struggle to get to the sewing machine.

"I have some thread and patterns. And even some old material you can have. I'd just like to see it go to a good home."

She sat at and pumped her feet, showing me how the treadle worked, and I watched the needle go up and down on the piece of fabric she held onto with her gnarled fingers.

"I should have asked earlier; what are you asking for it?"

"I was hoping to get twenty-five dollars for it. I paid forty for it years ago. Them things are worth almost eighty dollars now."

"Oh," I said, surprised.

"Well, what were you thinking? How much do you have?"

"I could pay you the twenty-five, but I only have ten dollars on me."

"Hmm," she said, sighing loudly. "Well, tell you what. I'll take the ten dollars, and you can make payments on the rest if I don't die sooner."

"Thank you so much," I gushed, embarrassed.

"I think there's still a sewing bee in town. Run by a woman named Gladys."

"Thank you," I said, again.

"Herbert!" she called out.

A few minutes later, a middle-aged man in stocking feet came in from another room.

"Yeah?" he asked.

"I jus' sold this sewing machine, and we need help getting it into this lady's truck."

Herbert picked the machine up like it weighed nothing, and I grabbed a box of patterns and the fabric and followed him outside. Baby Dorothy stood on the bench seat of the truck and looked out at us. She gave a shy wave to Herbert, but he either didn't notice, or he wasn't paying attention because I never saw him wave back. Even after he put the machine in the truck bed.

"Thanks so much," I called. "I'll be back."

On the way home, I stopped in at the grocers and asked his wife if she knew the woman called Gladys.

"Sure do," she said, writing down a phone number.

I called Gladys when I got home, and we got to talking. She welcomed me to the sewing bee and told me to bring some of the children's clothing I wanted to make. She said she had some fabrics she wasn't using, and she'd show me how to make patterns and use the machine when I was ready.

I asked my neighbor, Thelma, if she'd watch the children the next afternoon, knowing I'd have to trade her an afternoon with her three. I found Gladys' house where the women gathered. It was a much nicer area than where I bought the sewing machine, and I could hear the women talking and laughing as I walked up the cobblestones to the house.

"Come on in," Gladys called before I even knocked on the door.

She introduced me to the other ladies, and I recognized a few of them from going in to town.

"Put your things on the table, and I'll show you how to make your patterns."

Gladys showed me how to use a stitch-unpicker to undo the seams on the clothing I brought. I accidentally poked my finger a few times, and then I got the hang of it. She then had me iron the pieces, so they were flat enough to trace onto paper so I could reuse the patterns. I then cut those out and by that time, the ladies were done with their work for the afternoon and pouring glasses of iced tea.

"I'll show you how to pin those patterns on to fabric, making sure you're going in the right direction, and then you can go home and cut them out and bring them to our next bee," Gladys said. "But have some tea before you go. Myrt made us some cookies."

By the time I got home, my back was aching from bending over the table, so after taking down the laundry from the clotheslines, I did some ironing. Even though we had a clothes washer, doing laundry after we had guests was always a chore. Plus, I insisted the sheets were neatly ironed, for I'd learned from the laundress at the mansion and from the hotel down the mountain, it made them softer and smoother over time.

I'd gotten sidetracked today, what with the sewing bee, to ask Jack to go down into the icehouse and bring me a piece of the deer we had stored there. I'd ask him to do it tonight when he got home, so I could cook it tomorrow for our dinner. Since I'd run out of time for our evening meal, I cut up the rest of a ham and made a dish of bacon, tomatoes and lima beans. I put that on the stove to simmer while I drove the truck to pick up jack.

CHAPTER TWENTY

In 1934, Mr. Ferguson opened up the first movie theater on the mountain and everyone and their brother lined up all the way down the block just to get in. At the time, they didn't know there were only seventy-two seats available per showing, so some frustrated movie goers complained they'd waited in line for nothing when there wasn't enough room for everyone to get in. To appease his grumbling customers, Mr. Ferguson had the bright idea to have the ticket seller bring the tickets outside and once she counted to seventy-two, she put up a hand written A-frame sign that said "Sold Out." At least they didn't have to waste their time hoping they'd get in.

Being an enterprising man, he then had her start selling tickets for the next show, and told people they could come back. For the first week, every time we thought about going to the movies, the line to get in was still too long for us, and I worried Mr. Ferguson would quit showing the movie. But finally, on a Sunday afternoon, we left the children with our neighbor, and the three of us—Mother, Jack and I—bought popcorn, sodas and candy bars from the vendors outside, while we waited to get in. The movie was *It Happened One Night* starring Claudette Colbert, as a spoiled socialite who falls in love with a rascal played by Clark Gable.

Growing up, I'd only read about movie stars and now seeing them in a film just made them bigger than life for me.

"I'll bet they live in mansions like the Fletchers," I said to my mother as we left the theater.

"Ruth," she said, "you know they're only people. They're not so glamorous in real life. Just look at the Fletchers. They seem to have everything, but what do they really have besides money?"

Suddenly I felt like a child being scolded, not only for being infatuated with an imaginary lifestyle full of parties, romance and excitement, but for telling my mother how I felt. I would never have said anything like that to Jack. I was content with my life with him and the children, and I wouldn't have traded that for anything.

I then thought of how Mrs. Fletcher acted like she was above everyone in the household, yet was meek and passive with her husband. And then there was Mr. Fletcher, who acted as though his money gave him the right to take advantage of people. I hated thinking about him and how he most likely found a new young girl to charm.

As much as I tried to put those two contrasting lifestyles from my mind, I found I took those thoughts to bed with me that night. Then Jack reached over to kiss me goodnight and said, "Love you," like he did every night. A few minutes later, Mabeltwo climbed onto our bed and did her circle dance before she found the perfect spot between us.

That's when I could finally set those thoughts to rest. I couldn't be happier with my life.

———————

The years seemed to speed by as quick as lightning and it was 1941 before we knew it; Dorothy and Jack were in school, my mother still worked full time at the resort and had been promoted to Head Housekeeper and I started working there too. Bonnie and Clyde, and John Dillinger were killed, the Hindenburg burst into flames, and Amelia Earhart flew solo from Hawaii to the U.S. mainland.

And on December 7, the Japanese bombed Pearl Harbor, and we were at war with Japan and Germany. Jack had just turned fifty-one and was too old to enlist, or he would have done so at the drop of a hat.

"I need to do something," he said, despair in his voice.

"I'm sure there are things you can do to help," I said, grateful he'd be spared from the draft. There weren't enough eligible young men on the mountain to have our own recruitment center, but when I went to the grocer's I saw a flier on the bulletin board with tear off slips giving the phone number to an office down in San Bernardino. I brought one home and Jack immediately called them.

"One thing we can use," the recruiter told him, "is metals. More than likely, we're going to need everything we can get our hands on."

The minute Jack hung up, he said, "I've got a plan."

He had me post a note on the bulletin board.

Our Government Needs You!

We were flooded with calls and Jack told his remodeling customers he'd be fitting in time to collect and deliver metals and salvage for the war effort. He made a list of those people who'd called to tell him they had things for him, and he began scheduling trips to pick up what they had. Once the truck was full, he drove down the mountain to a scrap yard in San Bernardino.

I'd paid off my sewing machine several years ago, but I remembered seeing the widow woman's yard filled with junk when I'd first gone there. I knew she'd passed on, and when I drove by her house, I knew her son might still live there, for there was more junk in the yard than the last time I'd been by. Weeds grew through old tires, and I could barely see the tops of old batteries. Several iron chairs were stacked on top of each other, and an old rusty lawn mower that hadn't mowed a lawn in years had wildflowers growing through its blades.

I knocked at the door and Herbert, the son, answered.

"I don't know if you remember me, but I bought your mother's sewing machine several years back."

Herbert's eyes narrowed. I couldn't tell if it was from wariness or poor vision. Eventually he recognized me. "Oh, yeah," he said.

"I'm helping my husband collect metals and scrap for the war," I said, "and I'm wondering if we could come back and pick up what we can use from your yard?"

He thought about it, then said, "I was just thinking about cleaning it all up—it'll save me the trouble."

I wasn't about to tell him I knew differently; I wanted him to let us haul away what we could use.

"I'll take a few things now if you'll help me."

I opened the back of my station wagon, and Herbert filled it.

"Do you want us to call you when we can come back?"

"Nah, just take what you want. It'll save me."

"Okay, we'll be back. My husband's name is Jack, in case you see him. Don't go shooting him," I said half seriously.

"Ha! That's a good one!"

I could hardly wait to show Jack my finds when he got home. Instead of transferring everything to his truck, he asked if I'd mind following him down the mountain the next time he went down.

"I should be ready tomorrow," he said.

The next morning, I dropped my mother off at the resort, then made sure the kids got on the school bus. I followed Jack down to the scrap yard and the men there helped unload both our vehicles.

"While we're down here," Jack said, "want to have lunch at the diner? We could have hamburgers and a malt."

That sounded great.

"While we're here, we could stop at Sears and get you a new pair of work boots. I can almost see your toes sticking out of these," I said, pointing to his shoes.

"And I love you too," Jack said.

From then on, if I saw junk around, I'd stop and ask the owner if I could load it in to my car, and at least once a week Jack would load his truck with lead pipes, old batteries, junk car parts, brass casings and old plumbing parts for bombs, ammunition, tanks, guns and battleships. They would use the rubber tires for gas masks and life rafts. If there were old cars, he'd call the scrap yard to come pick them up. At the end of 1941, the government halted production of cars to save steel, rubber and glass.

In 1942, President Roosevelt ordered men between the ages of forty-five and sixty-four to register for non-military duty, and manufacturers stopped producing washers, refrigerators, sewing machines, record players and radios. With the children in school most of the day, I got a second part-time job at the bookshop in the village, which was still attracting visitors and locals alike. Clyde had taken over another space when a store owner retired, so there were twice as many books to sort and catalog. I was in seventh heaven. Clyde still let me put books on layaway and although he'd offered me an employee discount, I told him it was costing him money to let me make payments on books he might have been able to sell to customers at full price.

I'd never done bookkeeping, other than what I did for the cabins, but I started helping him post his sales and expenses into ledgers. Instead of combining them both on one journal page, I suggested he keep track of sales separately so we could add the columns quicker, and he let me run with my idea.

There were a few authors up in the mountains, and I suggested we do book signings and readings, and we offered a ten percent discount on purchases made at the event. We did them every month unless we were having a snowstorm, and we made a lot of extra sales.

"I think you were meant to be a bookseller," Clyde said one day.

"You know how much I love books, and I love what I'm doing," I said.

I then quit my job working at the resort.

During the spring and summer, when the Village was the busiest, we started opening on the weekends. While I missed spending time with Jack and the children, I started working those days as well. It wasn't that Clyde wasn't friendly with our customers, but he let them shop on their own. I, on the other hand, greeted them and reminded them if they needed any help, all they had to do was let me know. I found I was adding to our sales by recommending books similar to what our customers were buying, and each week, I'd change the displays in the store windows.

If we brought in a new book from the publisher, I'd put it on an easel on the check-out counter, along with five or six copies. Our weekend sales doubled. Ads in the local newspaper were expensive, but I talked Clyde in to doing one a month. Our part-time residents were up more in the good weather, and when they came in, a lot of them mentioned they'd seen the ads and had never known there was a bookshop in town.

I loved what I was doing and all my earnings went into our savings account.

We lost Mabeltwo that fall. She had suddenly developed a growth, and we thought she'd poked herself on something outside, but we couldn't find a puncture wound. It grew bigger, and she was becoming listless, so we took her to the vet, and it turned out to be cancer. I'd never heard of animals getting a disease like that, but the vet said it was more common than most people thought. I'd gone with Jack to the appointment, so we stayed while they put her to sleep. I'd loved Mabeltwo, but Jack took her death really hard. As with Mabel, she'd become a constant companion to him.

"What will we tell the kids?" he asked.

"We'll tell them the truth. Do you want to get another dog?"

"Right this minute, no, but I know I think we should."

"See if they want to go to the shelter with you, and they can help you pick one out."

That next weekend, Jack drove the kids down and his intention was to have the kids decide. But after looking at them all, he went to a pup that looked like our two Mabels, and when he reached down to pet her, she licked his face.

"This is the one," he said.

And they brought home Mabelthree.

CHAPTER TWENTY ONE

In 1944, the lack of rain and snow contributed to the dying trees and dry brush up in the mountains, and a fire broke out near the hotel where I'd worked when I came up here. As a volunteer fireman, Jack was called to go out. Fifty mph winds were feeding the flames, and we could see the black smoke blowing towards us from the other side of the mountain. It turned out no one was injured, and no buildings were destroyed.

I could only sigh in relief he was okay when I heard the tires on his truck crunching the gravel drive when he pulled in. Because they had their own system for washing their clothes, Jack left his sooty gear at the fire department, but every time he went out, he'd come home with soot still under his fingernails and caked in the creases on his face.

Not long after the fire, young James Thelen's parents posted a sign at the grocer's; his 1942 pickup truck was for sale. Word had spread that James had been killed while in France. Jack's truck had gotten to the point he was constantly doing repairs on it, and I knew he'd never suggest we buy him a new one. But with the money I'd saved, we could afford to buy James' truck.

I hated calling the Thelens under the circumstances, but when I mentioned we might be interested, Mr. Thelen said, "We hate to sell it—." I knew he meant to end the sentence with "because James isn't coming home..." and it broke my heart. I couldn't even bear to think about what I'd do if I lost one of my children.

We pulled Jack's old truck over on to the side of our drive, and put a sign on it, hoping someone would find some value in it; but after a couple of months of no one calling on it, we parked it to the side of the office so it wouldn't be the first thing people saw when they drove up to the cabins.

In 1945, President Franklin D. Roosevelt was elected for his fourth term. We were neither Republican nor Democrat; we just wanted the war to be over and to get our lives back to normal. And when we invaded Germany and dropped the second bomb on Japan, we saw the war finally come to an end.

That was also the year we got a real refrigerator from Sears, and moved our old icebox into my mother's cabin. Next to my wedding day and the children's births, it was the best day ever. There was twice the space inside, which meant I could bring some things up from the root cellar, so I didn't have to go down there so frequently. Right after Jack and I married, I'd gone down there to get something, and found the largest spider I'd ever seen, sitting in its web making a meal out of some poor bug. I was so startled I dropped the jar I was carrying, and thankfully it didn't crack open and spill its contents all over the dirt floor. What a mess that would have been! So ever since then, I didn't rely on the electric bulb hanging from the wire; I brought a flashlight to check every corner and crevice before I reached for what I'd come down for.

My mother still ate her main meals with us, often helping me cook, but now that she had the icebox, we got her a hot plate for her cabin so she could cook or heat something up if she didn't feel like joining us. We still had to have the iceman come, but she paid for him.

We hadn't celebrated Oktoberfest since the war broke out. Knowing people still despised the Germans, the Village decided it was time to celebrate, anyway, and we had what they now called a Fall Festival. For two weekends, the mountain celebrated with beer, food and live music. Vendors set up tents to show and sell their wares, and there were even a few carnival rides. We opened the bookshop on Saturday and Sunday, and even though that meant I'd worked seven days in a row, I didn't want to miss being there.

The bakery decorated cookies for us that looked like open books, and we served them along with a punch drink outside on a table decorated with fall flowers. Dorothy was fourteen then, and old enough to stand by the table and greet people.

"Don't forget to come inside and see the new books on display," I heard her say when someone came up to the table.

Over the next spring and summer, Jack began re-roofing the cabins—he'd found a leak in cabin number two the previous winter. I'd had to soak the bedcover in water, then vinegar to remove the stains from the wood ceiling.

Jack hired a young man named Robbie who'd helped him on larger jobs to pull the shingles off, and then load the back of the truck. On a roof job he'd done in the past, Jack did the bending and loading himself and he could hardly walk for about a week.

"I guess I keep learning the hard way," he'd said, wincing in pain.

Back then, he'd alternated a warm soak in the tub with ice wrapped in a towel, and yet now, I'd still occasionally see him take a break and stretch his back. He and Robbie finished two cabins and were starting on the third when I heard a loud cry coming from my mother's cabin. I rushed outside to see her bending over Jack, who cradled his left arm in pain.

"I think I broke it!" he cried out.

"What happened?"

"I wasn't paying attention, and I slipped off the roof."

Robbie was still standing up above us and called out, "You okay, boss?"

"Can you sit up?" I asked Jack.

"Give me a minute to catch my breath."

"I'll go get the keys to the truck, and then we're going to the hospital," I said.

For once, Jack didn't object. When he finally made it to his feet, his arm was dangling unnaturally and I could feel the blood drain from my face.

"Get in quick," I said, helping him up into the cab. "We should have taken my car."

He flinched with every bump in the road, and every time he did, my stomach went cold like I could feel the pain myself. A few hours later, with his arm in a cast, we headed back to the cabins.

"I'll need to pay Robbie to finish taking the roof off and then find someone to put the new one on. Can we stop at the lumberyard to see if anyone knows someone?"

The bulletin board was filled with names of men specializing in different trades, and Jack wrote down the number of one man he was familiar with.

"It'll take some of our savings, but I don't see another way," he said glumly.

He was silent the rest of the way home.

"We'll be fine," I said, patting him on the leg.

We finished my mother's cabin, then figured we could wait until the next year to do the rest of the cabins. Jack's new man, Johnson, and checked the other roofs to see if there was any physical evidence we might have any leaks, and he slipped some shingles in where he thought we could have a problem.

"That should keep you," he said.

"Thanks, Johnson," Jack said, handing over an envelope with cash in it.

Rather than sitting at home not bringing in any money, for the next few months, Jack took Robbie on the jobs they could handle. He made less money by having to pay him, but he kept himself busy and he kept his customers happy.

Clyde gave me another day at the bookshop, which helped.

That fall, we found a fox with a broken leg on the side of the road in to town. Rather than shooting it, we somehow managed to get it into the bed of the truck and we took it to a woman on the hill who treated injured animals and kept them if they weren't able to be released back into the wild. I'd heard about her, but I'd never been up there. Her name was Diane, and she lived in a trailer to the right of some fenced in pens that were home to a bear, a deer and a raccoon.

"Oh, how cute they are," I said in a tiny voice.

"You can't touch them. No matter how docile they seem, they're still wild animals. I have proof of what can happen," she said, holding up a bandaged finger. "Bring the fox in here."

She led us to an enclosed room equipped with a stainless steel table and all kinds of equipment, including a saw! Clamps, catheters, and other tools were laid out on the table against the back wall. I could smell the ether, and I could tell my face drained again. Not only did I feel strange, but Diane noticed it as well and asked if I was okay. I tried not to watch while an assistant gave the fox an injection that put it to sleep.

"We'll see what we can do. It looks like she'll be okay, and when you come back up, you can see her in her new home. I don't imagine you'll have rabbits, rodents or frogs on hand, but bring her some apples, pears or grapes. We'll make sure she has her protein," Diane said.

"This is an amazing place. And you obviously care about these animals."

"We got a bobcat last year. Our first goal, after treating the injuries, is to get these guys back out there. But some are just too vulnerable if they're not a hundred percent, so those are the ones we keep."

"Where do you get the money to do it all?" I asked.

"We have volunteers, like Dr. Jensen here, and we take donations, both money and food."

"Can I bring our children up when we come back?"

"Of course. Maybe they can volunteer on the weekends."

"Oh," I said, surprised. "That would be a great experience for them. You can meet them, and then decide if you think they'll fit in. I'll casually mention it so they won't be surprised when we come back."

We went back to visit our fox the next weekend, and both Jack Jr. and Dorothy loved seeing the animals. I'd only told them the reserve survives on donations and volunteers, and when Diane offered them jobs, Wildhaven had two new volunteers.

The bowling alley had been under construction for over a year, and finally, in 1947, it opened just in time for Dorothy's sixteenth birthday party. She wanted to have a slumber party and invited five of her girl-friends from school. There was no way we could accommodate five extra people, not to mention giggling girls in our cabin, so I ran it by Jack before I told Dorothy they could stay in one of the cabins. We had plenty of cots, and I figured my mother could listen and keep an eye out for me.

We barbequed hamburgers and hotdogs, before we dropped the girls off at the bowling alley, and since we'd told Jack Jr. he could have a friend over, they wanted to go too.

"As long as they don't bug us," Dorothy said.

When they returned, they wanted to roast marshmallows and s'mo-res, and Dorothy made it clear Jack and his friend weren't invited. It made me a little nervous for them to be out there with the fire, but Dorothy knew enough to cover the pit when they were ready to go to bed. It also helped that Jack volunteered to check it out, too.

I thought for certain they'd be tired of each other by the next day, but Dorothy asked if they could stay one more night in the cabin. They wanted to go have pizza. I'd originally planned to have our family din-ner, but I figured she only turned sixteen once, and I wanted it to be a birthday she'd always remember. Pizza sounded good to us too, so we all went down to the pizza parlor, and we made sure we sat on the other side of the restaurant so the girls could have their freedom.

On Sunday, everyone slept in, and then we made a big breakfast be-fore the girls went back home. Dorothy helped my mother make dinner, and afterward, she opened her gifts. We'd bought a necklace with a gold "D" on it, and Jack Jr. got her a new book she'd asked about. My mother gave her a scrapbook going back to when she was a baby. She'd been working on it for almost a year, going to the library looking up events that happened during Dorothy's lifetime, and finding old newspapers and magazines she could cut up and paste to its pages. Every birthday and special event was documented with photos from albums I'd kept, and the last ten pages were left empty, waiting to be filled in with her life until she reached twenty-one.

CHAPTER TWENTY TWO

On Dorothy's eighteenth birthday, she announced she was going to go to college. It was 1949, and there was a large demand for teachers. It meant she'd have to drive up and down the mountain every day to go to classes, or she'd have to move down to San Bernardino. Either way, we needed to buy another car, and while neither Jack nor I wanted her to move away, it made more sense for her to do that than to do so much driving. She enrolled at the community college, and when she found out one of her good friends was also going down, we found them a small house they could share. We filled it with furniture from the secondhand store, and we made a list of all the food, cleansers and other cleaning supplies she'd need to get started on her own. During that summer, we found her a 1946 Ford sedan, and I went through my cupboards and shopped here and there until I had everything she'd need. The week before school started, we filled the truck and her car and we all drove down to get the girls moved in.

I was her age when I came to the mountains, and I'd promised I wouldn't cry. But seeing my beautiful daughter putting her things away in the new house tore at my heart. I made the excuse of needing to find the bathroom down the hall so I wouldn't embarrass her with my tears. When I came back, their radio was on, and the girls were in their own little world. Jack was breaking the moving boxes down, and Jack Jr. was helping him with the trash.

The three of us climbed back into the truck and we began our trip back up the mountain, but not before I blew my nose and leaned my head against the passenger window so I could close my eyes.

"I know. Let's stop for a malt," Jack said cheerfully.

My eyes were still closed when I imagined sitting in front of a thick chocolate chip malt, and as hard as I tried, I couldn't keep a tiny smile from forming. The minute Jack Jr. saw it, he cried, "Yes!"

We sat in a booth and while we waited for our malts, and fries for Jack Jr., he talked about how cool it was going to be to have the house to himself.

"I can get my own record player and not have to share dessert."

"Now don't forget, with Dorothy gone, there will be more chores," Jack said.

Jack Jr.'s shoulders slumped noticeably, and I couldn't help but shake my head at him.

The first night Dorothy was gone, I found myself going to her bedroom to check on her before we went to bed. I tried to imagine she was spending the night with a girlfriend, rather than coming to grips she was not coming home for a while.

When it was time for us to go to bed, I called to Mabelthree.

"C'mon. Snuggle with me so I won't miss Dorothy so much."

The next morning, I made Jack Jr. a huge lunch and added extra chips.

"Next year, I want to leave campus with the other guys for lunch," he announced as he climbed into Jack's truck.

I finally talked with my mother about how lonely I was feeling, and she sounded like she'd been preparing this talk, for she had lots to say.

"Remember, you raised your children to become adults, and while you never experienced the excitement of going away to college, just imagine how it must feel to believe you can do and achieve anything you can dream of. Plus, she's missing you all too, but in a different way. She might be lying there at night, thinking about being at home, where she's safe, but then the excitement of it all takes over again."

"And," she continued, "even though Jack Jr. acts like he doesn't need you, he still does. Do things with him, or have Jack include him in something they both can do. Parenting is not for the faint of heart."

And when I talked to Jack about it, he was also very positive.

"She's not that far away, and we can always go down and take her to the store every now and then. And Ruth, you need to give yourself a lot of credit for raising such a fine young lady."

"I think you need to give yourself a lot of credit, too," I said to him. "You've been a wonderful dad to both the kids, and it shows. I just feel like the house is empty, but I'll get over it."

"Good night," he said, patting me.

"Good night."

Even though Jack Jr. was still at home, I felt a part of me had been cut away. Our house seemed empty without Dorothy. I had to learn to make less dinner, or I'd find myself with too many leftovers. Jack was good natured while I was often melancholy; Jack Jr. didn't seem to even notice his sister wasn't there.

I had finally adjusted to the change in our family dynamics, when the next year, Jack Jr. told us he also wanted to be a teacher and would like to enroll at the same college. The girls agreed they could tolerate him as a roommate, thus saving us from having to find them a larger house. Because Jack Jr. would have to sleep on the couch in the living room, we bought him new sheets and pillows. It wasn't much on looks, but we found him a dresser and a portable clothing rack.

For some reason, I didn't struggle as much with Jack Jr. leaving home as I did with Dorothy; I don't know if it was because I'd already gone through the heartsickness of a child leaving home. I also didn't worry so much about his safety. He still had so much to learn, but he was a boy, and boys were supposed to be able to take care of themselves.

We took him shopping, like we'd done with Dorothy, and made sure he had plenty of all the snacks he'd eat. While we shopped, we picked up enough food and supplies to line Dorothy's cupboards, too. Before we dropped him off at the house, we stopped at Penney's and bought him some new shoes and clothes. He wanted to be sure he wore what all the other boys down the hill wore.

On the days when I missed them the most, I had to remind myself I wanted to see them mature and get an education.

As my mother reminded me, "You raise your children to be strong and independent, so let them be both."

Sometimes thinking about that didn't make me feel any better.

In 1950, the malt shop opened in Cedar Glen, and Jack turned sixty. He didn't want to make a big deal out of it, but he wanted the kids there, so they drove up. We invited about twenty friends for hamburgers, fries, malts, and dancing to the jukebox. We spent over a hundred dollars that night, but it was worth it to see Jack be at the center of the evening. I'd asked everyone to write down something funny they knew about Jack, and one of his friends read them all out loud. We'd said no gifts, but people brought cookies, and the children bought him a new toolbox.

That Sunday, we packed up my mother and the kids, and we drove in to Big Bear to have a picnic lunch, then stop for ice cream. It was an unusually warm day for Big Bear's higher elevation, but we all welcomed the sun. We stopped in a few stores, and I bought Jack a new bone-handle single blade buck knife with a leather sheath at a shop that sold Indian handicrafts.

"That's a pretty fine knife," Jack said when he opened the wrapping. "Almost too fine to use. Thanks, Ruthie."

Dorothy graduated from college and married a young man who wanted to move back to his hometown of Bakersfield to teach. I tried to reason with myself that it wouldn't be so terribly far away that I wouldn't see her, but logic doesn't always prevail when your heart hurts a little.

Jack Jr. decided he didn't want to be a teacher after all and had one more year before he became an aeronautical engineer designing airplanes.

I turned forty in 1953, and I wanted to go down the mountain to San Bernardino. The county fair was going on, and it'd been years since we last went. Dorothy and her new husband drove out for the weekend, and to save Jack Jr. the trip up, we planned to pick him up on the way down.

We had cotton candy, popcorn, hot dogs, and my mother and I sat and watched as Jack and the kids rode the bumper cars and the tilt-a-wheel. I thought for sure someone would get sick, but no one complained about having a stomachache.

We watched couples dancing to the country music, and Jack and I even danced a couple of slow songs. We went to the petting zoo and saw the rabbits, goats and some ponies. The auction was right next to the zoo, so we watched as pigs, sheep and calves were auctioned off.

"You know they sell those animals to slaughterhouses," Jack said, out of earshot of the kids.

I'd never thought about that, and my stomach sank when I thought about the children who'd raised them—did they know where their beloved pets were going to end up?

By the end of the day, we were exhausted. We dropped Jack Jr. off at his house, and then we started the trip back up to the mountain.

The sight of the old hotel on the highway always reminded me of my trip up to Lake Arrowhead with Charlotte and Clara, and while it seemed like a lifetime ago, it always made the hair on my arms stand up. Of course, then, I had no idea what I was going to do, and I never thought my life would turn out like it had.

I turned to look at my mother dozing in the back seat and, as I often did, wanted to apologize for taking so long to let her know I was all right so many years ago. Dorothy and her husband were still awake. I looked at Jack's profile. Gray hair was weaving its way into his temples, and his beard was almost completely gray. His skin was tanned from working out in the sun, but he still only had a few laugh lines around his eyes. He could tell I was looking at him, and he smiled. He reached for my hand.

"Are you happy?"

"More than I ever thought," I said, squeezing his hand back.

Who would have known my life as I'd known it was never going to be the same.

CHAPTER TWENTY THREE

A new fire broke out near the Village and it was big. Even before Jack got the call, we could smell the smoke from as far away as our cabins. Jack quickly dressed in his fire clothes and gathered the gear he always kept ready near the front door.

"Be careful," I called to him as he climbed into his truck.

"Love you," he called back.

By the time I said "Love you," back, he'd closed the truck door, and I knew he'd never heard me.

He was gone all that night and the next day. I knew it was a bad fire, for we could see enormous clouds of smoke from the cabins and the sky had turned a pale gold. Ash was falling on my car and I grew more worried every hour that I didn't hear from him.

I didn't go into the bookshop the next morning, knowing everyone would be staying off the roads. Eventually I heard from Jack. He was all right, but the fire had gotten out of control. Fire crews came in from all over the county and they were hopeful it would make a change for the better since the wind had died down.

My heart beat fiercely as I listened to him, wanting him to be home with us, but knowing he was bound to his job and to helping others. When he didn't come home the next day, I worried he'd been working round the clock and wondered if he'd slept. The unwritten rule was that no one rested until they put the fire out.

I tried to sew to fill my time, but my hands shook so badly I had to stop. I tried to read, but I couldn't focus on the words and I found I was only re-reading the same words over and over again. When the air began to clear, I could tell the fire was getting under control. I'd barely slept the last few days myself, and my nerves were shot. All I wanted to do was crawl into bed with Jack by my side and sleep for a week.

The third night, just as I was dozing in my reading chair, I heard what I'd been waiting for; the crunch of gravel as Jack's truck pulled in. I jumped up, knocking the book to the floor, and ran to the door.

But as I opened it, I saw it wasn't Jack's truck—but that of someone I didn't know. Even in the dark, I could see the truck was red and there were lights across the roof. Though they weren't on, I knew this was a bad sign.

My first instinct was to run out to the truck, but I knew I needed to steady myself—to brace myself for what was to come.

I glanced over at my mother's cabin and watched as she made her way to us.

"Ma'am," the fireman said, taking off his helmet. "There's been an accident."

Jack was dead.

My mother's hands were warm and strong as she took my arm. I looked at her for a few seconds before I turned back to the soot covered man who stood in front of us.

"What happened?" my mother asked.

"He'd gone into an evacuated home and the homeowner hadn't removed all his firearms and ammunition. While he and another volunteer were in the house, bullets started exploding and the shrapnel killed both men. When the other firefighters realized what was happening, they had to back off on any rescue attempt, but they continued trying to put the fire out."

I covered my face with shaking hands, then tried to take in a deep breath. My chest tightened like someone was squeezing me—I tried to calm myself by taking deep breaths. My lungs felt hot like I'd been in the fire myself, and I suddenly couldn't catch my breath. The harder I tried, the worse it got, and the fireman quickly pulled up one of the Adirondack chairs outside so I could sit.

"I'll get some water," my mother said, rushing into the cabin.

My mind and body were numb. I fell into the chair. I'd heard everything, but my brain wasn't processing anything.

Jack couldn't be dead.

My mother returned with a cool glass of water, and I quickly drank it.

Gripping his hat, no doubt eager to leave, the fireman said, "If that's all, ma'am, the department will have more information for you tomorrow."

How could he just leave me?

I waited for the numbness to fade.

Around an hour later, my mother looked at her watch and said, "I'm worried about leaving you. Do you want me to call in to work tomorrow?"

"No. Go in." I said. "Now, I'd like to sit outside a while longer."

"I'll stay with you tonight," she said. "And we can call the children."

She left to go get a change of clothes from her cabin, then took them inside before rejoining me outside. Eventually we went back inside and I just dropped into bed without changing in to my nightgown. Mabelthree laid up against me, sensing something was off.

"It'll be all right in the morning," I said to her.

But of course it wasn't.

My mother made coffee and toast, but I just sat at the table in a daze. I followed her to her car, and gave her a weak smile.

"I'll be fine," I lied.

The moment she drove out our drive, I went back inside the cabin. It was a warm day, but suddenly my hands were ice cold. I stood in the doorway for a minute, just looking around the office and at the details of everything; the leather sofa, the painting over the fireplace, my bookcase filled with books, and when I saw the phone on the counter, I thought maybe this had all been a nightmare of some sort, and I waited for the phone to ring. Surely someone would be calling me to tell me it was all a misunderstanding.

I closed the door and leaned against it, but found myself slumping to the floor. I didn't have the strength to get back up. I tried to breathe. The silence was deafening and then I felt a ringing in my ears. The tears came; my eyes welled up and I couldn't help but cry.

Part Two

CHAPTER TWENTY FOUR

After Jack's funeral, I wandered aimlessly about the property, trying to find comfort in the woods that used to bring me peace. When that didn't help, I retreated into my cabin, hiding from the world. Every time I heard a noise, I turned to see if it was Jack. When I did that, Mabelthree would lift her head and look in the same direction, and I wondered if she sensed him there too.

Dorothy and Jack Jr. stayed in their old bedrooms, and with them still there, I quickly began feeling the warm rooms were suffocating me. For a change in scenery, I found myself at the top of the steep slope down to the creek that flowed behind the cabins. The distinct smells of the forest—the leaves, the fallen and decomposing tree trunks, and the pine trees themselves. The blankets of moss covering the ground added their own musky sweet smell. I closed my eyes and took in a deep breath, trying to allow all these scents to revitalize me, but no matter how hard I tried, I couldn't, or *wouldn't*, let them in.

I turned toward the hammering of a woodpecker. In all the years I'd been up here, I'd never seen one close up, and I hoped today I'd get a glimpse. When the rhythmic drumming stopped, I turned back around, and somehow lost my footing and tumbled down the ravine into the creek. I was more surprised than hurt, and it took me a minute to get my bearings and to check to see if I'd broken any bones. I caught my breath and then quickly realized that although the air around me was warm, the creek water was icy cold. I got up, and that's when I realized I'd hurt my ankle. I looked up the embankment and wondered how I'd make it back up.

As far as I knew, Dorothy and Jack were still in the cabin. I knew my mother was at work, but I called out to all of them, anyway.

"Dorothy! Jack! Someone!"

I groaned in pain as I tried to stand, and I let myself fall back down. As much as I struggled, I knew I wouldn't be able to walk back up. Crawling on my hands and knees, I inched my way upward, until, exhausted, I let myself sit back down, and that's when I began to cry. I could die out here and no one would know where to look for me! Or maybe I *should* just die and my pain would go away.

Realizing I was being idiotic, I wiped my runny nose on my sleeve, rolled back over into a crawling position, and continued my journey to the top. When I finally got there, curling smoke from our chimney told me the kids were up.

"Dorothy! Jack!"

Finally Jack Jr. came out the door and looked first toward my mother's cabin, and then to where I was standing, propped against a tree.

"I fell," was all I could say before I started crying again.

He quickly called for Dorothy, and they both ran to help me. Once I made it inside the office, I iced my foot and then Dorothy wrapped it in an Ace bandage. The cabin was beginning to smell like a funeral parlor from all the bouquets of flowers we'd brought home, so I asked her to get rid of some of them and open all the windows. I spent the next few days in bed with my foot propped up and Mabelthree lying beside me. Every now and then she'd whimper and let out a deep sigh, then rearrange herself so her head would be on Jack's pillow. Each time she did that, a trace of Jack's woodsy cologne moved gently through the air, a constant reminder that he was gone.

Dorothy found a pair of crutches at the secondhand store so I could eventually get around, and I'd at least have the freedom to go outside again if I chose to.

While there was a void in my heart again to see my children leave, I also felt a little relief they were gone; I couldn't have faced this last week without them, but I was tired putting on a happy face and pretending I was doing okay.

The next week, the silence hit me like a brick. I'd had my fill of daytime television and reading, and was going stir-crazy. Plus, I'd never felt so alone. Every time I heard a vehicle on the gravel, I thought it was Jack's truck. We'd never been able to sell his old truck, so I hung a For Sale sign on one of the trees, hoping someone would see it as they drove by. I would keep his other truck for now.

I often slept with the last book Jack bought me, *Pride and Prejudice*, by Jane Austen. He'd written a note and tucked it inside rather than writing directly on the book page:

For Ruth Ann Maynard.

My wife and my rock.

With Love, Jack

I might have been his rock, as he referred to me, but he was the wind beneath my wings!

I called Clyde to let him know I'd be coming back to work.

When the weather turned warmer, the dogwoods bloomed along the roads and in the ravine behind the cabins. Wild rose bushes clustered on the ground and some branches had climbed up a tree. I thought they'd be a welcome greeting to our guests in the gardens in front of the cabins, and had always meant to ask Jack if they could be transplanted. I'd just have to do it and find out later if they made it.

I missed my Jack Maynard!

The bookshop was my only salvation. No sudden noises startled me like they did at the cabin; the conversations with customers were light-hearted and helping them find a particular book stopped me from thinking about my problems. At home, I'd be lost in my own thoughts, often forgetting what I was doing, and sometimes finding myself doing something twice. Here, though, I could pull out books, smell their pages, read the first few pages, or skip to the back and read the ending.

At night, I lay in our bed with Mabelthree; I could at least pretend Jack was still there, especially when I'd wake to the sounds of coyotes calling to each other. As Jack once explained it to me; they were either calling their pack together after hunting, or they were staking their territory, and warning other coyotes against trespassing. Mabel's ears would perk up, and a sound between a cry and a growl would emanate from deep inside her.

We had more guests than normal after Jack's death. It was both a blessing for the income, and a curse, for all the extra work it created for me. I took Mondays off from the bookshop so I could do the laundry; I washed the sheets and hung them on the clothesline to dry. Most of the time, the process went smoothly and without incident, but one Monday, after a very busy weekend with guests, I had three sets of linens to wash and hang. The wind whipped the sheets one way and another, and I tripped on one as it fell. I went down with it, pulling another sheet down on top of me. Suddenly, I felt trapped and panic-stricken. I cried out and flailed about, causing myself to become more entangled in the sheets, and unable to figure out which end was which.

No one was there to free me, so I lay there for a few minutes, until I envisioned someone coming upon me and seeing me in this tangled mess. Suddenly it struck me as being funny. I began to laugh uncontrollably and then I realized how ridiculous this whole thing would look: me tangled and laughing almost hysterically, and it made me laugh harder.

I laughed so hard, I coughed phlegm, then peed my pants.

Eventually, I relaxed and rolled over a few times until I could figure out a way to free myself.

I hadn't hurt myself, but the entire ordeal wore me out. I brought the dirty sheets back in to the laundry room so I could wash them in the morning before I went to work.

It seemed laundry and I weren't on the same page for the rest of the month. One morning I'd hung a few loads on the line before I left for the bookshop, and the minute I left, it started to rain. I'd learned to recognize the smell of upcoming snow as I'd learned to smell rain, and sure enough, after the rain we had a light snowfall. It quickly turned back in to rain, and all I could think about was that laundry and the day I got caught up in those sheets. I knew the laundry would be drenched, and I didn't even give it a look see when I got home; it would just have to hang there until the weather changed.

Rain fell over the next few days, and only a few die-hard customers were willing to venture out. I took that time to address postcards to customers on our mailing list, and to work on the bookkeeping. All in all, we were doing well, and I knew Clyde would be pleased.

I could tell he was slowing down, as he rarely came into the book-shop. I made all the bank deposits, and each day before I closed, I'd fill in the day's sales and expenses, so if he did decide to come in while I wasn't there, he'd be able to quickly see how we were doing.

I was surprised how minutes would pass when I didn't think about my sorry situation, and the hours and days still went slowly as I longed to see Jack—to hold him in my arms.

My Jack.

Each night when I soaked in my tub, I wondered how I was going to manage without him. Mostly I'd get lost in my own thoughts, only realizing how distant I'd become when one day, Dorothy called me and we got talking. All of a sudden, she asked me something, and I hadn't even heard her. I had quickly gotten into the habit of feeling sorry for myself when Dorothy or Jack Jr. called. It seemed like our conversations were always "woe is me." I realized I was dragging my children down with me. I tried to think about what my mother would do—she was always so calm and rational. Then it came to me; she'd grab the bull by its horns and make the best of the situation.

If we were going to survive, I had to be strong—for me, but also for Dorothy and Jack Jr.

"I'm sorry," I said to Dorothy.

"What?"

"It looks like it's going to be a beautiful day today."

It had dawned on me that not only was the sun out early, but the promise of a new, brighter day was right there in front of me. As soon as we hung up, I went outside to breathe in the mountain air. Off to my left, I saw an expansive white owl fly across the road and disappear into the forest behind us. I'd only seen one once before, and I remembered Jack telling me white owls symbolized transformation and change, and if you saw one, that meant you were going to have good luck.

CHAPTER TWENTY FIVE

Even with my newfound optimism, in the months that followed, I thought about cleaning out Jack's clothing and dresser drawers, but I couldn't do it. My eyes would well up with tears, just at the thought of it. On one such attempt, though, I did find his old five-gallon water jugs filled with spare change on the floor of our closet. They were so heavy, I had to tip them over on to the floor and transfer the change into smaller buckets. Our bank had a machine that separated and counted the coins, and I got a whopping two hundred dollars for my trouble! If I was a gambling woman, I would have gone to Las Vegas.

Time passed as it always does, and even though the afternoon sun shone through the cabin windows, I was chilled to the bone. I wondered if it was because I'd decided to visit Jack's grave. Later, as I stood beside the only man who'd ever shown me love and tenderness for all those years, I thought about Jack's funeral more than a year ago.

The small chapel was filled and before the service began I glanced to the back, and I saw that some people had to stand. Dorothy chose *Amazing Grace* for the song, and afterward, she, Jack Jr. and I sat in the front pew as everyone passed by us giving us their condolences.

The neighbor women set up tables and chairs outside the cabins, and served lunch for us and for whoever wanted to stop by afterward. I watched as Mabelthree anxiously greeted everyone, searching for Jack among them. She finally gave up, and softly whined as she came to sit by me. The whole ordeal was thick with awkwardness for me. When I looked at all the people gathered there, it was like we were suspended in time. Some people talked quietly, and others carried on lively conversations. How could they do so at a time like this?

Later, as everyone was leaving, the only thing I could say was "Thank you for coming."

Afterward, I went into the cabin to be alone. After helping clean up, eventually Dorothy, Jack Jr. and my mother came inside. It wasn't long before I went back outside to breath the clean air, and I begged the whisper of the trees to surround me with the calming nature of the mountains. Bent over, with my hands on my thighs, I let myself cry and I could see tears drop on to the leaves of our old oak tree. Mabelthree came to my side, and I petted her.

"I know girl," I said.

Despite my sorrow, birds celebrated the day with their songs, and I resented them for their happiness. I was grateful no one came out to cheer me up. I wanted to be anywhere but there. I remembered that day like it was yesterday.

And now, here I was a year later. I was finally ready to bring myself to start going through Jack's things. For a moment, just seeing his clothes in our small closet, or in his dresser made me believe he was still here with me. But I was ready to let the material things go. A new family shelter had opened in town, and I filled three bags of folded pants, socks and shirts and brought them in to them. Hopefully, they'd find some men who could wear them.

I threw away most of his old shoes, but a lot of his jackets were good enough to donate. I kept his one heavyweight Pendleton shirt for myself. We'd buried Jack with his wedding ring. He didn't have any other jewelry, but I found the buck knife I'd given him years ago, still in its box. I remembered him telling me it was too nice to use, and I was sorry he'd kept it in that drawer. But then I thought about the many times he'd lost his work knives and had to buy new ones at the lumberyard or hardware store over in Cedar Glen. Maybe he was right after all. I put the knife back in the empty drawer; perhaps I'd give it to Jack Jr. for Christmas.

I had Robbie help me push Jack's old truck out and put a For Sale sign on it. Somehow, I'd forgotten about the old wooden Chris-Craft boat Jack had wanted to restore.

"I know, I know," he'd said. "I have too many projects and not enough time. But it could be a project Jack and I could work on," he'd said wistfully.

How could I say 'No' to that, when he'd provided for us all these years?

"I'll have to go see the boatman," I told Robbie. I took some Polaroid pictures of it and I went over to Cedar Glen, where the boatyard was.

"You're lucky you caught me here," Jacob McCallum said. "I have another yard over in Big Bear and I'm only here a couple a days a week. Let's see what you got."

I watched Jacob in silence as he studied the photos. He pursed his lips and scrunched this mouth in concentration.

He said, "Well..." as he scratched his beard in thought. "I'll bet your husband is sad to see this go. It could be a beauty when it's restored."

"My husband died last year," I said solemnly.

I'd surprised him with my frankness, and I saw he was caught off guard.

"Oh—," was all he said. Then, "I'm sorry."

He reached out and touched my arm. I could feel the warmth of his hand through my shirt.

"I could lie and say it's okay, but it isn't. He died in the big fire last year. He was a volunteer fireman. Had been for years." I tried to stop them, but tears stung my eyes.

"I'm really sorry," Jacob said again. "You got kids?"

"I do—Dorothy and Jack Jr."

Jacob McCallum's kind eyes searched my face, and then set on my teary eyes.

"Seeing as it would make a fine boat if it was restored—can I come by and see it? I mean, when you're ready?"

I sighed. "I'm as ready as I'll ever be. I need to clean it and Jack's old truck out. We have cabins we rent out and it would tidy up the property."

We made arrangements to meet the next day he was coming back to town. That gave me a few days to have Robbie give the boat a good cleaning. That next Tuesday, I was cleaning cabin number six when I heard him pull into the property. My stomach sank a little when I saw the truck and attached trailer. If he did indeed buy the boat, a part of Jack would be leaving me today. I could just tell it was going to happen.

"Hey there," I called out as I approached his truck.

Another man climbed out of the passenger side.

"Ruth, this is my helper, Joe."

"I forgot to tell you the boat was on a trailer," I said.

"I see it. I guess I forgot to ask. Let me check her out and see if we can just bring her back on that one."

Jacob turned to Joe, who was looking the boat over from head to toe.

"Looks good, boss," he said.

"Would you take three hundred for her?"

Joe turned his head in surprise. Although I had no idea what the boat was worth, I knew Jacob was being more than generous with his officer, and it was hard for me to not jump at his offer and say 'yes.'

"It'd be fair for both of us," Jacob said, as though he needed to convince me. "And while I'm here, maybe I can take that truck off your hands."

"Boss—," Joe said.

Jacob held up his hand. "How's about a hundred for the truck?"

Now I *knew* he was being way too generous; I was close to paying someone to haul it away.

"I can use it for parts."

I looked at Joe, who was chompin' at the bit to put his two cents in. Jacob took his wallet out and counted out four hundred dollars.

"Joe, help me take this trailer off so we can hook the other one up."

"Come inside when you're finished," I said, "and I'll write you out a receipt."

About half an hour later, while I was back doing laundry, I heard the bell over the office door jangle.

"You've got quite a place here."

"Jack had it before we got married," was all I could think to say.

"Do you get a lot of guests?"

"We do pretty good. Sometimes we're a lot busier than others. I also work at the bookshop in the Village, so I stay pretty busy."

"Well, I won't keep you then," Jacob said, his smiling eyes warming me a little. "I'll let you know when I can come back to get the truck and my trailer."

"Thanks, Jacob," I said sincerely. "I know you're doing me a favor by buying that truck, and I really appreciate it."

I was disappointed I didn't hear from Jacob that next week. Robbie had come over to clean the truck, and although I knew it wasn't worth much, I wanted it to look as good as it could. I'd bought a dozen mixed cookies from the bakery, thinking Jacob could stay a few minutes and have some with me, and I realized I was disappointed I wouldn't have the companionship of someone else, even for just a few minutes.

CHAPTER TWENTY SIX

I sat at our empty kitchen table, remembering when the kids were still younger and how they'd either tell us about their day, or sulk if they were in a bad mood. I'd remind them to eat their vegetables. Then I thought about Jack and me sitting there after the kids had left for college; how I'd sometimes bring home something from the sandwich shop across from the bookshop if I was running late. Or how he sometimes made something simple for dinner.

Now Jack's chair was empty—there was no one to make plans with or to share the events of the day.

I ended up cutting the cookies in half and putting them on a plate; I took them to the bookshop for our customers.

That next week, when I was cleaning cabin number five, I found some mouse droppings under the kitchen sink. The only way I knew how to get rid of mice was to set traps, but I wasn't about to do it myself. I bought the traps and peanut butter and called Robbie.

"You know, if you have mice here, you might also have them in the other cabins. We should probably set traps there too, and I can come back and check them every day," he said.

One other time when we'd had mice, Jack told me this silly saying; "You know the early bird gets the worm, but the second mouse gets the cheese," and I always thought it was funny. I told Robbie, and he just looked at me like I didn't know a thing.

We caught quite a few mice in the traps that week, and part of me felt sad for them; I hated to see any animal die, but we couldn't have them scaring guests and chewing up our place. When we set traps in my mother's cabin, she suggested using either peppermint oil, cinnamon, or vinegar to keep them away in the future. I wondered if she knew that from living in the mansion. While we were at it, I also had Robbie do a thorough inspection of the cabins, looking for and sealing up any cracks in the log exteriors with caulking or steel wool, and replacing any of the old weather stripping. I added yet another chore to my list of things to keep up with.

A few weeks later, Jacob McCallum called to apologize for not getting back to me sooner, and to see if he could stop by and pick up his trailer.

"I also want to see if I can start the truck."

"It's been years since we drove it," I said.

"Are you going to be around next Tuesday?"

"I just hired a new girl for the bookshop, so I'll put her down to work for me."

"Good. I'll come by around ten?"

"I'll have coffee ready. That is, if you drink it?"

"The darker the better," Jacob said.

"See you then."

On Monday, I made sure to bring some banana nut bread home from the bakery so we could have something to eat with our coffee. I found myself getting a little nervous that Tuesday morning; I put on eye shadow and did my lips. I started the coffee at nine-thirty and warmed the bread before I cut it and set it out on the table. The office smelled delicious.

Ten o'clock came and went, and I was getting fidgety. I didn't have anything to do, and trying to concentrate on a book was impossible. What had gotten into me? At ten forty-five, I heard a truck pull into the drive, and I peeked out the window. Jacob was by himself, and he backed his truck right up to his trailer. He got out and moved the trailer slightly so he could hook it up. Then he jumped on the hatch and when he was satisfied, he jumped back down and wiped his hands on his pants.

He was done in ten minutes, and here I'd thought he'd be interested in some coffee. It looked like he was all business. I felt my face flush, then he knocked on the door and when I opened it, I felt myself flush even more.

Mabelthree rushed to see who it was, and when she saw it was Jacob, she wagged her tail with excitement.

"You all right?" Jacob asked. "Hey there," he said, reaching down to pet her.

"I'm good. I was just doing my chores and got a little warm," I lied.

"Well, I'm all hooked up."

I looked outside like I hadn't already seen him out there.

"Did you want to have a cup of coffee? At least I can do that for you," I said, pointing to the table.

"I'll take you up on that."

We sat at the old pine table, and with our coffees and bread, there was an easy silence between us.

"How long you been up here?" Jacob finally asked.

"About twenty-three years now. Are you originally from here or Big Bear?"

"Neither. I moved to Big Bear first, when I started my boat service. Since it's not a private lake lots of people come up every year. Then I saw a need for my service in Arrowhead and opened the shop there. But I'm originally from the Los Angeles area. My folks had a dairy down there. When we came up one summer vacation, I knew the mountains were where I eventually wanted to live. After my divorce, it was a perfect time for me to make the move. Plus, I loved boats, so I found my profession."

Jacob looked around a bit, and then said, "With your children out of the house, it must get lonely for you then—up here."

"It does sometimes. But my mother stays in one of the cabins, and I have Mabelthree," I said, reaching over and petting the dog as she lay by my chair.

"*What's her name?*" Jacob asked, tilting his head as if to hear me better.

"Mabelthree. Mabel the third. We couldn't think of a name we liked better when the first Mabel died, so we ended up with Mabeltwo. When she died, Jack went back to the animal shelter and he brought back our girl, here," I said.

"Hey, Mabelthree," Jacob said, and her ears perked up. She looked at me, then got up and sat by Jacob and gave him the sad eyes.

"She's looking for a handout now," I said.

"Well, she's found a sucker," Jacob said, breaking off a piece of his banana bread. "Well, I'd better get going. When should I come back and get the truck?"

"Any time is fine. Just let me know."

"Will do. And thanks for the coffee."

I saw Jacob to the door and stood there watching as he climbed up into this truck. He turned to wave before he closed the door. The trailer creaked a little as he pulled it away.

The next week, he called to tell me he and Joe could come out that next Tuesday and pick up the truck.

"I guess if I'd known we'd be back so soon, I could have left the trailer here," Jacob said. "Oh well. I'll see you around ten?"

I bought cookies from the bakery and made some coffee for the two of them, and a little after ten, I wondered if he was going to be late again. The weather was decent, so instead of sitting there and waiting for him, I did a load of laundry, and was outside hanging it up when the two of them pulled into the drive.

"Sorry we're so late, Ruth. We have us a fawn in the back of the truck."

"A fawn? As in a baby deer?"

"Yup. We saw its mama dead alongside the road, and he, or she, was just standing there next to her."

Joe said, "We had to drag the mama back off the road, and it took both of us to catch that little thing."

"We tied its legs up and wrapped it up in a blanket. As soon as we get the truck loaded up, we need to figure out what to do with it."

I immediately thought about Diane at Wildhaven and said, "I know exactly where to take it. I'll give Diane a call and tell her we're coming up."

Before he had a chance to say more, I ran inside and made the call. I came back out as they were using the winch to get the truck onto the trailer.

"Whew," Joe said.

"If we can get the fawn into my truck, I can drive it over to the preserve," I said.

"Joe, do you mind taking the truck and trailer back, and I'll go with Ruth?" Jacob asked.

"Sure thing, boss," Joe said. "I'll help you get it into her truck."

Once the deer was settled, I went inside and locked Mabelthree up in the office. I set the time on the plastic clock face sign on the door to let anyone who came by know that I'd be back later in the afternoon.

"Have you ever been there?" I asked Jacob as we drove.

"No. I've heard about it, though, and I'm looking forward to seeing it."

"Jack and I brought a fox up there several years ago, and Diane's vet fixed her up and now she stays there. Can I stop at the store to get some apples?"

"You're driving."

"I know, but I don't want that baby to be afraid any longer than she has to be."

"She'll be fine."

When we pulled up, Diane was there to greet us. She and Jacob got the fawn out and Jacob carried it to a pen that Diane had prepared.

"Is it hurt?" she asked.

"No ma'am," Jacob said. "Just lost its mama."

"Well, let's get her settled." Diane turned to me and said, "I see you brought fruit. Thanks."

Diane took Jacob on a quick tour of the facility, and our fox was still there. I hadn't been up for the last few years, once the kids left to go down to college. It looked like there were a few more animals, including a gigantic bird and another raccoon.

"This one's named Bandit, because he steals the food before we can get it to him."

"He's very handsome," I said.

145

"How're the kids doing?" Diane asked as she walked us out to my truck.

"They're good. I sure miss them around the house."

"And I'm real sorry to hear about Jack. I know it's been a while, but I haven't seen you."

"You know, things get a little better every day," I said. "I still miss him terribly, but I'm keeping busy with the cabins and working at the bookshop. Thank goodness for that."

"Well, don't stay a stranger. And when the kids come back up to see you, be sure to bring them by. I miss them. They were good helpers."

Diane and I hugged.

"Take care," she said.

"You too."

On the way back down the hill into town, Jacob said, "I don't know about you, but I'm starving. Can I buy you lunch?"

I hadn't realized I was also hungry and said, "That sounds great. There's a little restaurant in Cedar Glen."

"It's around the corner from my boat shop," Jacob said, and I suddenly felt silly.

"Hey, Jacob," one of the waitresses called out as we came in. "Iced tea?"

"You bet. And you, Ruth?"

"Iced tea sounds perfect, too."

"Need menus?"

"Ruth might."

Although I studied the menu, I ordered the turkey sandwich with fruit, which is what I'd had the last few times I was in there. Jacob ordered a club sandwich and fries.

"Well, we did our good deed for the day," Jacob said, taking a sip of his tea. "I'm glad you were there to help me."

"It actually felt good to get out of the house and do something to help someone—or something," I said.

I watched as Jacob took a bite from his sandwich, then poke two fries into his mouth. It looked like he'd recently cut his hair, for it was short and trim, and I guessed him to be in his late forties or early fifties. It was hard to tell someone's age when they worked outside for the weather aged their skin. When he looked up at me, I suddenly looked down at my plate. I hadn't meant to stare.

"So how'd you come to live in Lake Arrowhead?" he asked.

I told him only that I'd worked for a wealthy family in Seattle, and when I decided I wanted to do something else, I moved up to the mountains. He nodded as I spoke, and if there were any doubts about my story, he didn't let on.

"I married Jack, and we lived happily ever after until he died fighting that fire," I said with an empty laugh, and even I could tell it rang false. I changed the subject. "I've grown to love these mountains. The minute I decided to stay, I felt a sense of belonging. It was as if I could take a deep breath and all the weight of the world would lift off my shoulders."

"I think everyone who lives in the mountains feels that way." Jacob chuckled. "I've also come to think everyone who comes up here and stays, comes to start over. I was still down in the Los Angeles area, married—I thought happily enough—when my wife took up religion. Now, I'm not saying religion is bad, mind you, I'm just saying, sometimes I can be critical. She started goin' to church every Sunday, then she joined a bible group, then she sang in the choir, then she got on committees for the potluck, for the Christmas pageant, and what not."

He stopped to take a sip of his tea.

"Well, one day, she told me she wanted a divorce. She told me she'd met someone else, and that he treated her real nice. Now, I had no idea she was unhappy, but then again, all I did was work. And after dinner, I'd go out into the garage and putz around with my boat. So I guess I wasn't payin' enough attention to her. When I thought about it, it served me right."

Jacob studied me for a moment, and then said, "It turned out to be the preacher."

CHAPTER TWENTY SEVEN

In September, the leaves began to change color, the days grew shorter, and the nights turned cold. The year Jack died, we'd planned on replacing the gas wall heaters, but we never got around to doing it. The old floor heater in the office still took longer to heat, and the bedrooms always seemed to stay cold.

I asked at the lumber yard if they had the name of a heating man and a few days later, someone came out to give me a price to do the work. Two days later, my new heater was installed and the office and bedrooms were nice and toasty.

Most evenings, I'd sit and read by the fireplace until my eyes drooped, then Mabelthree and I would climb into bed; sometimes if she fell asleep before I did, her snores and twitches would keep me awake. When she did that, I'd gently pet her, and she'd stretch her legs and fall back to sleep.

In October, Clyde came into the bookshop and told me he wanted to retire.

"My daughter and grandkids live in Redlands—I really don't want to leave the mountains," he said sullenly. "It's where I made my life."

"I can understand. I wouldn't want to leave now either." I was afraid to ask, but I needed to know how this would ultimately affect me. "What will you do with the store?"

I was sure he was going to say he would close it; there was no way he could run it from so far away. The store had been a lifesaver for me, and now I'd have to find somewhere else to work for I needed the income. Working in the bookshop had given me purpose and the will to go on. How could I ever live without the books? I tried to stop thinking about myself and put myself in Clyde's shoes. I understood his daughter's growing concern about him being up here by himself. What if he fell, or worse, had a heart attack? There would be no way she'd even know, maybe before it was too late.

We were both in a pickle, and I felt a knot tighten in my stomach.

"Will you open a new store down there?"

"I've given it a lot of thought. I looked at some places, but I just don't know if I have the energy to move all this. There's a bookshop down there now, in the downtown area, and they want to sell. The folks are not much older than me—" his voice broke miserably. "I could come up a few times a week if I had someone to run the store for me."

It was impossible to hide my disappointment. I was grateful there were no customers in the store, for my heart wasn't into talking to anyone right then. I sat at the counter, a heaviness weighing me down, knowing my life was about to take another turn for the worse.

"Or I could sell it if I knew someone was interested."

"I suppose you could put an ad in the newspaper," I said solemnly. I sighed deeply and imagined myself looking in the paper for my own 'help wanted' ads.

"If the right person came along, someone I knew who loved these books as much as I did..."

Clyde went into the office, and fiddled with his paperwork. He looked at the deposit from yesterday. "It'd sure be a shame to close it."

When a customer finally came in, I tried to avoid eye contact, fearing the weight of my disappointment would be so obvious to them.

"Good morning," I said.

"I've come for the book I ordered."

After a minute, I recognized Mrs. Wishman, and said, "Let me see. I have it right here."

I unwrapped *The Catcher in The Rye* by J.D. Salinger and scanned the description before I put it on the counter. Mrs. Wishman flipped through the pages as I wrote it up.

"It should be a good read and I love that it's been quite controversial," she said, smiling mischievously.

"Do tell me what you think of it," I said out of habit.

Thankfully, Mrs. Wishman's visit distracted me, and as she called out her goodbyes to Clyde, I took another deep breath. At some point, I was going to have to deal with my new predicament, but for now, I wanted to free my mind of any such thoughts.

I closed the cash register drawer and made my way to my favorite part of the store, where the old books filled the bookcases. I instinctively inhaled their musky fragrance. I was compelled to run my fingers along their spines as I dawdled, realizing there were so many books I'd never have time to read if Clyde closed the store. Oh, how I would miss this place!

Clyde found me and stood watching me for a moment.

"Well, what do you think? Are you interested?" He raised his eyebrows in expectation. "I called out to you."

"Are you asking me if I'm interested in carrying on with the bookshop?"

"Of course, Ruth. Who else did you think I was talking about?"

I sometimes felt I was the densest person on the planet. I didn't know what to say. Of course I would love to have the shop.

"But I don't know anything about running a business," I protested.

"Ruth, who do you think has been running it for the last few years? Without you, we wouldn't have been able to survive."

"Yes, but..." I stammered.

My heart said yes, but my rational side said, "I don't think I can afford it."

When I got back to the cabins, my mother was home, and I knocked on her door.

"What should I do?" I asked, after telling her about Clyde's offer.

"I think you should do it. I have some money set aside and I could become your silent partner."

At the end of October, Jacob McCallum called me up and told me he'd decided to restore Jack's old truck rather than scrap it.

"It's not that I need another project," he said. "I think when I'm finished, she'll be a beaut."

Taken aback, I quietly asked, "But, have you started working on the boat yet?"

"Well. . . I've done a little here and there, but I've been taken with the truck."

I wasn't certain why, but my stomach lurched when I heard him say that. I knew when I sold it to him, it wasn't mine to have a say, and I thought he was going to tear it down like he'd said. Now, he was going to rebuild it, and I might one day see in on the road.

"You think it's worth it?" I asked quietly. If he noticed the despair in my voice, it wasn't obvious.

"I haven't seen one around up here for a while, so yeah, I do."

I was lost in my own thoughts when Jacob said, "Ruth? Are you there?"

"I'm here. I was just surprised, is all. It's fine."

"I didn't mean to upset you. I wasn't thinking. I never should have said anything."

"No, honestly, Jacob, you're fine, and it will make a fine truck for you. Jack and I always loved it."

The first week in November, I became the proud new owner of Books & Co. I knew it was taking a chance, but I decided to have our grand opening Thanksgiving weekend. It gave me plenty of time to advertise, and the holiday was always a busy time for the mountain.

Thursday morning, Dorothy came out from Bakersfield, where she taught second grade; her husband had appeased his parents and driven to Oregon for the long weekend. Jack Jr. and his new wife, Susan, drove up from San Diego, where he'd landed an internship at an aeronautical school. We'd booked all but one cabin for the long weekend and I wanted to leave it open for any unexpected guests, so everyone stayed with me.

Mild November weather was cooperating with us, so Jack Jr. took his wife and Dorothy to the Village so they could watch the boats and feed the ducks. Afterward, they went to a matinee at the movie theater. My mother and I cooked. After dinner, Jack Jr., Susan and Dorothy cleared the table and did the dishes, while I put the leftovers into the new Tupperware bowls I'd bought at a party a few weeks ago.

"These are great," Dorothy commented as I showed her how to push on the lid to release the air.

I made myself a mental note to order her some for Christmas.

After we finished putting everything away, we stoked the fire in the fireplace and watched the movie *White Christmas* on the television. We were all yawning by the time it was over, and when my mother left to go to her cabin, I was ready for bed. The night air had chilled, but it was a perfect mountain evening. The moon was still bright, and from a distance, it looked like the tips of the pine trees were glowing in the sky.

"Come on in, girl," I said to Mabelthree. "Time for bed."

Friday morning, I left the kids a note that they could either make their own breakfast, or go to the coffee shop with the twenty dollars I left for them. I'd left early to go to the bookshop. I was nervous about Saturday's open house and I wanted to make sure everything was neat and dusted. Julie, who worked part time in the shop, had offered to come in early also, but I wanted some quiet time to gather my thoughts.

I made a list of everything I needed to do; dust, make sure the books were in alphabetical order, check with the bakery to make sure they had my cookie order, and when Julie got there, go to the bank to have plenty of cash in the register. I still had to go to the grocers to get sodas, Dixie cups, paper plates and napkins, and then to the printers.

The kids drove up to Big Bear for the day, and were going to have dinner there so I had a quick bite to eat at the sandwich shop before I went home. I was tired, but I'd gotten everything done I needed to, so I took a hot bath, and then read by the fireplace before heading off to bed.

On Saturday morning, the first thing I did was look outside to make sure the kids' car was there, and breathed a quick sigh of relief to see they'd returned safely. I still had a ton of things to do in the store, so I left them another note, but this time with no money. They were old enough to figure out what to do for breakfast.

My biggest project of the day was to arrange the 'New Books' table, and I ended up redoing it twice before I was happy with it. I unpacked the box of bookmarks the printer had done up for us as a gift and set small stacks of them around the store. Everyone who purchased a book would get one too. I found a spot on the counter for customers to sign up to be on our mailing list.

My mother and the kids got there early to set up. While my mother went through the store again, dusting and straightening everything out, Jack Jr. set up the tables outside and Dorothy and Susan put the cookies on platters and arranged the refreshments. I chewed my cuticles and tried to relax.

The open house started at four, and at three-thirty, Clyde got there. Right behind him, Jess Campbell and her sister Ida arrived. While they were checking out the refreshments, I rushed to touch up my lipstick.

"Hi ladies," I called out as I approached them. "Help yourselves to some goodies, and check out our newest books."

Alice Harris, Marie Turner and Betty Stewart greeted each other as they came in, all with a glass of punch in their hands. It hadn't occurred to me to request that nobody bring in their drinks, and I was praying there wouldn't be any accidents.

"This is my mother, Dorothy," I said as I introduced my family. "And these are my children, Dorothy and Jack Jr."

"Well, nice to meet you all." Marie Turner said.

"And Clyde," Betty Stewart said, "We're sure going to miss you."

Clyde had found us in the crowd.

"You'll be in good hands," he said, patting me on the shoulder like I was a young child.

I excused myself and said hello to a few more customers. I checked in with Julie, who gave me a thumbs up before she started writing up the first sale. My mother was trying to help a customer find a particular book, and I felt so fortunate to have my family here to support me.

"You don't need to hang around," I said when I caught up with Dorothy and Jack Jr. "Why don't you take Susan and Grandma to the malt shop like we used to, and have hamburgers and malts?"

They looked at me like I'd just had the greatest idea ever, and nodded.

"Julie and I can clean up when we're done," I said.

Just then, a woman holding a small Yorkshire Terrier came up to me. She looked vaguely familiar, but I couldn't place her.

"Ruth?"

"Yes."

"Look at you, owning a bookshop and all."

"I'm sorry. I recognize you, but I can't recall your name," I said, trying to concentrate.

"It's Vivian Hayes."

"Oh my gosh," I gushed. "Ms. Hayes. I had no idea you were still up here."

"You mean, it's been so many years, you didn't know I was still alive and kicking," she said pleasantly.

"It's wonderful to see you again. Do you live up here full time now? Are you still making movies?"

"No, I'm too old for that. No one wants to see an old lady on the screen. But I still come up for a while, then go back down to Los Angeles. It looks like you've done well for yourself. I'm so proud of you. I never heard back from you, and I hoped you were all right."

Suddenly, my mind burned with the memory of my last day working for her and a terrifying thought washed over me. She and Jack were the only two people in the mountains who knew I was pregnant! If my panic registered with her, she didn't show it, and instead, she kissed her dog.

And then I remembered she was kind to tell me to look her up after the baby was born, and her driver took me to a place he knew would hire me as a housekeeper. Patrick was his name.

I gathered my composure and said with the clearest voice I could, "I have two grown children now, and I still love living in the mountains."

She seemed almost oblivious to what I'd just said.

"It's hard for me to read a lot now, but I still love books. So I'll look around and see if there's anything I can't live without. I'll see you before I leave, but I wanted to make it a point to say hello."

Just as I watched Vivian Hayes walk away, I saw Jacob McCallum standing there with the largest houseplant I'd ever seen. When he saw me, he lowered the plant and I could see his face had turned red, and a sheepish grin filled his face. I couldn't help but smile, and I could feel my face flush.

Old Mrs. Baldwin came to me and was asking me if we had any new Agatha Christie books.

"New or old?" I asked.

"New, of course."

I took her to the mystery book section and waited impatiently while she went over the list of books she'd already read.

"There. I don't have this one," she said, taking a book off the shelf. "I'll take it."

I walked her back up to the counter and saw that Jacob was still standing there patiently.

My mother hadn't left with Dorothy and Jack Jr. yet, and as I approached him, my mother caught my arm.

"We're running low on cookies. I wondered if you wanted me to go to the bakery and get more before I go."

Then she turned and saw Jacob. He was shifting the plant from one arm to the other.

"Oh," I said. "Mother, this is Jacob McCallum. He's the man who bought Jack's boat and truck."

She looked from me to him, and then said, "Nice to meet you, Jacob."

"Same here, ma'am."

"Looks like a dandy of a plant," she said, taking it from him. "I'll find a good spot for it." She walked away, but not before looking at me askance.

"How did you even know about the open house?" I asked.

"I saw your ad and wanted to see your new store."

"Are you a reader?"

"Not as much as I'd like to be. Do you have anything *manly* you could recommend?"

"Follow me."

I led him to the mystery section.

"We have a newer James Bond book by Ian Fleming. *Casino Royale.* It came out a few years ago, but it's very popular with the men."

"Thanks. I'll give it a try." He gave a nod to the store customers. "Looks like it's a success."

"I was afraid no one would come because of the holiday. And there had been predictions of rain."

"Ruth," a customer then said. "If you have a minute, I'd like to get my grandchildren some books. I was thinking about Nancy Drew and the Hardy Boys?"

"Those sound perfect, Roberta. I'll show you where they are and you can decide which ones you'd like. Another customer who buys books from a particular author makes a list of the one's she's already read, so that might be a good idea for you to do with the grandkids. That way, you don't duplicate your purchases."

"That's a wonderful idea, Ruth. You young people are so smart."

"Ha," I said.

Before I could get far, Mrs. Wishman caught me and wanted to fill me in on the details of *The Catcher in The Rye.*

"Well," Jacob said. "I'm keeping you from your guests—anyway, could I take you to dinner after it's over?" He colored slightly.

Was he asking me on a date? I actually liked Jacob—but I hadn't given any thought to dating again. Maybe I was making more of it than it was. If the kids and my mother were gone, I didn't see any reason why I couldn't go with him. He must have mistaken my silence for a rejection, for he added. "I mean, since I'm already here and hungry."

"I'm hungry too—sounds good."

CHAPTER TWENTY EIGHT

Around seven, after everyone had left, Jacob hung around and helped Julie and me clean up. I took the cash out of the register and hid it and the receipts in my desk drawer; I'd do my paperwork in the morning before I opened the shop.

When we were finished, Jacob asked, "Where do you want to go?"

"There's a new sandwich place here in the Village—and we wouldn't have to drive in the fog. It looks like it's coming in pretty thick. And fast. Or there's an Italian restaurant nearby."

"Why don't we get a quick sandwich? I'm headed back to Big Bear, and hopefully it won't get much worse by the time we're finished."

"Sandwiches it is."

I closed the shop, and we walked across the way. There was only one other couple in there, so we almost had the place to ourselves. Once we ordered, Jacob fiddled with his straw wrapper. I had a habit of playing with mine too, and when he noticed, he chuckled.

"So how are you doing, Ruth?" he finally asked.

"I think I'm doing fine. Definitely much better than when I decided to sell the boat and truck. And having the bookshop has definitely brightened up my world. It's truly been a blessing."

"Nothing like work to take your mind off of things."

"And my kids came up for the open house, which made me feel good. It's been wonderful seeing them, and I'll hate it when they go home. But I have my mother. And I'm a pretty strong woman, so I'm making the best of it."

I smiled like I believed it.

"Plus, I have Mabelthree to keep me company at night. Sometimes I even bring her to work with me and customers love having a shop dog."

"I have one too. Name's George. He's a mutt, but a good dog."

"Where do you stay when you're in Arrowhead?"

"I rent an old cabin near the shop."

"That makes sense," I said, fiddling with my straw wrapper.

"That way, I can work late if I need to and roll out of bed early."

Jacob McCallum was easy to be with—I enjoyed his company, and if he was trying to court me, he was going about it in the right way. Slow and easy.

"You're lucky you still have your mother. How long has she been here? I don't recall seeing her the times I came by."

"She came down when the kids were young. She works as a maid at the resort now. What about your parents?"

"My dad walked out on us when I was a kid, and we never heard from him again. My mother remarried before I came up here, but she's gone now. Cancer of her lady parts."

He shrugged, but I could tell the memories still disturbed him. A sadness showed in his face.

"I still miss her," he said.

I forced a smile. "My father died when I was young. It was a railroad accident. But my memories of him aren't very great. He was a drinker, and he hit me and my mother."

Jacob's hand touched mine.

"I'm so sorry."

I shrugged. "It was so long ago, and once he was gone, I missed him less and less. It was a blessing." I looked at Jacob, then said, "I hope you're not disappointed in me for saying that."

"I'm not." He said. "I'm sorry you had to go through that."

To change the subject, I asked, "So, do you have children?"

He shrugged again.

"We never had kids—I would have liked a family. You're very fortunate there, too."

"Speaking of which, you missed them at the open house."

It seemed we'd run out of things to say, so we sat comfortably. I closed my eyes and said, "Well, I'm exhausted. It was a good day."

"I'm glad I could be here."

He looked outside, then said, "It's getting pretty bad outside. The Village is covered in fog. I should get going."

I knew the fog would be worse as Jacob drove out onto the ridge, so I said, "I hate to see you try to drive home in this mess. I have an extra cabin if you want to stay at my place."

Jacob's mouth twisted in thought, and then he said, "I think I'll take you up on that offer, if you don't think your family will mind."

"They'll be fine. If you can, follow me home. I'll drive slow so you don't lose me."

The kids were home when we pulled up in to the drive, but the only light on was in the office. For some reason, I quickly doubted the wisdom in my decision to have Jacob stay with us. What if they, or worse, my mother, thought I was bringing him home with me for other reasons than the weather? It didn't matter that I was certainly old enough to do whatever I wanted, but I almost felt eyes upon us as we got out of the vehicle.

"Stay here," I whispered. "I'll go get your key."

When I opened the door to the office, it was cold inside, and I noticed the bedroom doors were closed. Even though it was early, I hoped everyone had gone to bed. I let Mabelthree out and quickly grabbed the key.

Again, as the gravel crunched under our feet, I worried someone would peek their head out and see us, but it was so foggy I could hardly see the windows of the cabins. And even if they did look out, they wouldn't know who it was.

It was cold inside his cabin, so I started the fire in the fireplace and turned the wall heater on to speed up the warming process.

"I'll be making breakfast for the kids in the morning if you want to join us," I said, turning down his bed like he was a paying guest. I stopped, embarrassed.

"Thanks, but I'll probably get up early and head back home. Don't want them to get the wrong idea."

He must have been reading my mind.

As I turned to leave, I said, "Oh, and thanks again for coming out— and for the beautiful plant. I'll try not to kill it right away."

I turned and said, "And get a good night."

When I got back to the office, Mabelthree was right behind me, eager to get out of the cold air. I should have turned the heater on when I came in to get the key, but I was so nervous about what everyone might think, it slipped my mind. I couldn't help thinking about the day: the turnout was beyond my expectations, and I could hardly wait to add up our sales.

I wondered if I should have invited Jacob in to pass the time. It was too late to go back to his cabin now, plus I didn't want to give him the wrong idea. I looked outside the door to the office, and the fog was now so dense I couldn't see three feet in any direction. No matter what anyone thought, I'd made the best decision encouraging Jacob to stay.

It was too early for me to sleep, so I quietly bundled up in front of my fireplace and just stared into the flames. Mabelthree nudged my arm to give her a rub, and it amazed me how uncomplicated a dog's life was. If only my life was so simple. I also couldn't help but think of Jacob telling me he had no children. Even though mine had left to begin their lives, they were my life. And all I wanted for them was to be happy and successful.

Eventually my eyelids grew heavy, and Mabelthree and I headed for bed.

I woke to the smell of bacon cooking and coffee brewing.

"Thought you could use a bit of a sleep in and a hand this morning," my mother said.

Like a child, I stood in the doorway to the kitchen, rubbing my eyes, then tying the band on my robe.

"Smells wonderful."

"I see you have a guest."

"What?"

I let Mabelthree out and saw that Jacob's truck was still in the drive. I felt as though I turned ten shades of red, although I didn't have anything to be embarrassed about. I quickly turned and started a fire.

"It was so foggy, I didn't think it was safe for him to drive back to Big Bear, so I suggested he stay in one of the cabins," I said, still facing the fireplace. "He said he probably wouldn't be here for breakfast—I'll go get dressed."

When I came back out, Jacob was sitting at the kitchen table, drinking a cup of coffee.

"I changed my mind," he said, turning to look at me.

"Jacob was just telling me how he came to stay the night," my mother said.

"*Mother.*"

"Just giving you two a bad time," she said.

"Well, I'm hungry, and Jacob probably needs to get back on this way. I'll finish making the pancakes."

"Can I help with anything?" Jacob asked.

"Syrup is in the pantry and napkins should be in there too," I said.

My mother poured orange juice and water and set glasses out on the counter for the kids when they eventually made their way in. No sooner did we sit down to eat, when Dorothy came into the room.

"I'm starving—," she started, and then stopped when she saw Jacob. Her smile faded.

He stood.

"Dorothy, this is my friend Jacob. He bought Dad's boat and truck, and you just missed him at the bookshop yesterday. He lives in Big Bear, and it was so foggy, I told him he should stay the night and go home in the morning."

There.

For the longest time, she looked like she wasn't buying any of it.

"Don't be such a prude," my mother said. "You can make yourselves pancakes."

When Jack Jr. rolled in, he took one look at Jacob and said, "Hey."

CHAPTER TWENTY NINE

Before Jack died, we had talked about pushing out a wall to make room for a proper refrigerator and stove for my mother's cabin—but it was one of the many things on our list that never got done. There was no way it could be a surprise for her, so I had a contractor come out and give me a price to do the remodeling. I talked with the kids about it, and we all agreed that instead of them coming up and exchanging Christmas presents that year, they could spend the holiday with their in-laws and if they wanted to, they could chip in for the addition. Mostly, it was my mother and I who financed it, but we wanted the kids to be included.

I'd reassured my mother that Jacob and I were just friends, and asked if she minded if I invited him over to do either Christmas Eve or Christmas Day with us. It would just be the three of us. Other than teasing us during Thanksgiving weekend, she'd never given me any sign she had a problem with having him around. When I invited him, he sounded genuinely pleased. He'd been following the progress of the add-on and offered to lay the new linoleum floor.

"That's way too generous," I said. "I didn't know you were so handy."

"I've always liked doing things with my hands. Just have the materials there, and when I leave, you'll be able to have the appliances delivered. The boat shop won't be busy then, so it's actually a good time for me to be away."

"Bring a change of nice clothes," I said.

He came out on Christmas Eve day and worked until we were ready to go to dinner. I splurged for a buffet at the resort, and the three of us drove into the Village. The enormous tree in the lobby was lit and elaborately decorated, and I was temporarily transported back in time to the mansion with its large tree in the entry hall and when I first saw it, I involuntarily shuddered.

"Are you all right, Ruth?" Jacob asked.

If my mother felt any thoughts from the past, she didn't show it. Then I remembered Mr. Fletcher hadn't forced himself upon her, either, so her memories of the holidays were different than mine. I quickly pushed my thoughts aside. I wanted to enjoy my evening out, and I didn't want to bring anyone else down with me.

It surprised me the number of people having dinner out. I said hello to customers from the bookshop, and even the mayor was there with a group of about twenty people. After a filling dinner and an assortment of shared desserts, we headed back home complaining about eating too much.

My mother gave me a hug and went to her cabin, and as I opened the door to the office, Mabelthree bolted outside. Jacob and I went inside.

"I'll start the fire," I said.

"Sounds good. It's really getting cold."

Only minutes later, Mabelthree scratched at the door and whined.

"We could watch some holiday movies if you'd like. And if you don't want to drive back to your cabin tonight, you can stay here tonight."

I thought I was going to die right there. I couldn't believe it came out that way!

"I meant in one of the cabins," I said, cringing.

"I knew what you meant, Ruth, and I'd like that," Jacob said with a quick smile.

We watched *It's a Wonderful Life*, with Jimmy Stewart, which Jacob had never seen. After that, I made hot cocoa, and we watched the *Lawrence Welk Show* until Jacob started nodding off.

"I think I'm ready to head for my cabin," he said.

I rose early on Christmas morning, and made Jacob, my mother, and me breakfast. The floor in her cabin was almost finished, so Jacob worked on it until the early afternoon. After an early dinner, he and I left to go see *To Catch a Thief.*

We watched coming attractions and a newsreel before the movie started, and just before it did, Jacob took my hand and said, "You know, Ruth, I've really enjoyed the time we've spent together."

I didn't know what else to say, so I said, "Me too."

"I've been trying to figure out when to give this to you," Jacob said as we walked to my car.

In his hand was Jack's Remington Boy Scout pocket knife in a sheath.

"I found this, along with some old dog biscuits and a leash in the '32 Ford," he said.

My breath caught.

I knew Jacob was growing more interested in me and I wasn't fighting it. When you've lost someone you've loved, it's sometimes seems impossible to see a smooth road ahead of you. Like seeing a light at the end of a tunnel and it's not another train coming at you. But eventually, the dust had settled, and my pain had started to fade. Grief continued to surprise me in subtle ways; a television program Jack looked forward to, like *Gunsmoke*, would come on, and at first I could not watch it. After a while, I quit avoiding it, and I found I began to look at it again. I'd even catch myself saying something like "Jack would have liked that," or "Jack would have laughed at that" when something reminded me of him.

Or, I'd pass someone on the street who wore the same aftershave he wore and I'd breathe in the scent and if I closed my eyes, I could see Jack in my mind. I began to learn that from grief, it's not all pain. I tried to learn to appreciate the man he'd been; his kindness, his love for our children—and for me. And I began to learn I could live with a grieving heart.

As I got to know Jacob more, I could picture a life with him. He was a good man, a hard worker and sensitive, even though he wouldn't have agreed. And when he called to see if I wanted to do something for

New Year's Eve, I knew we were going to take the next step in our relationship. I was certain this was what he was intending; he was looking for companionship, no matter how we made it work.

I closed the bookshop early, knowing we wouldn't have many customers after noon. I'd been anxious all day, and I appreciated the break that the few customers who'd come in had given me. I brought the receipts and cash back into the office so I could make up my deposit. When the doorbell jangled, I came out as Mrs. Wishman came in.

"I came to pick up my new book," she said cheerfully.

I unwrapped *My Cousin Rachel*, by Daphne du Maurier and then gave it to her so she could glance through it as I wrote up a receipt.

"I should bring you some of my books to resell," she said, "but I can't bear to part with any of them."

"I know how you feel," I said. "I'm that way too."

"Well, I'm off, then. I'll end the year with a new book."

"Happy New Year," I said.

"And same to you, my dear."

I bolted the door behind her, then I made a quick deposit and locked it in my desk. I really needed to find a better place to hide my cash.

I checked in with my mother before I went to my cabin. I wanted to remind her I was going out and that we'd most likely be late getting home.

"Ruthie," she started.

Although it had never been her nature, I thought she was going to lecture me on being careful with the cold evening, and with Jacob. But she only gave me a hug and said, "Have a good time, honey."

I let Mabelthree out and left the front door ajar while I rooted through my closet to find the perfect thing to wear. I realized at the eleventh hour, I should have taken the time to shop for a new dress. Jacob had seen me in everything from work pants when he came to pick up the boat and truck, to nicer clothes when I was at the bookshop. But New Year's Eve called for me wearing something special. I still had plenty of things he hadn't seen me in, but that didn't make me feel any better about my lack of choices.

I finally decided on a pair of wool slacks and a cream-colored button down blouse, and laid them out on my bed. I could feel the cold air coming through the front door, so I made sure Mabelthree was on her way back in and once she was, I closed and locked the door behind her. I drew a warm bath and before I got in, I pulled my hair up in a clip. I soaked for a while, and when Mabelthree came in to check on me, she licked the moisture from the arm I had resting on the tub.

"Thanks, girl," I said, washing my arm off.

I spent some time doing my makeup, mostly lipstick, blush and mascara, and tried wearing my hair a couple of ways before deciding to wear it up in a combination twist and bun with a few tendrils strategically hanging down in front of my ears. I felt by wearing a drop of cologne Jack had bought for me years ago was in somehow betraying him, so I instead opted for a fragrance I found the last time I'd gone down to Sears.

I was nervous, but ready for Jacob when he arrived not long afterward. We took my car, and I watched him mutter aloud as he familiarized himself with all the workings of it. He gave me a sheepish smile when he accidentally turned on the windshield wipers, then pressed too hard on the brakes as we pulled out of the drive.

We had reservations at the Antler's Inn in Twin Peaks and as we drove up, I could see the parking lot was filling up. A series of cabins, similar to mine, were off to one side. It had originally been built as a dance pavilion, with log walls and huge logs beams spanning the width of the ceiling. The band was already playing soft music, with a catchy beat that made me want to dance.

The hostess seated us along one wall and handed us our menus. A waiter dressed in black pants, a tuxedo shirt, and bow tie was right behind her and took our drink order. I hadn't had a drink in years, so I asked for something light; a white wine. Jacob ordered a beer.

We were in a perfect spot to watch as more people filled the tables, and soon, a few brave souls got up to dance. When Jacob asked if I wanted to join them, I said, "Maybe after I have another glass of wine. I haven't danced in so long, I'm afraid I've forgotten how to."

We ordered prime rib, mashed potatoes, creamed spinach and creamed corn. I asked for everything to be served separately, and Jacob told the waiter, "Just put it all on *my* plate. It all goes into the same place."

Dinner was delicious, and I was on my second glass of wine when Jacob stood and reached out for me.

"Ready to dance?" he chuckled. "I can't promise I won't step on your feet."

The moment I was in his arms, I felt it. His nearness sparked the heat between us, and I was shocked at my reaction. A rush of pink warmed my face, and Jacob smiled playfully. To avoid eye contact, I drew closer to him, which meant it was easier for him to bring his cheek to mine and I could feel my heart pound.

Gently, he rocked me back and forth to the music, and I found I naturally followed his footsteps. I could feel the warmth of his hand on the small of my back, and the firm but gentle grip of my hand wrapped in his was almost electric.

He whispered, hot against my ear, "I've waited for this moment for months."

I felt I was sinking into his embrace, and for a moment, I thought how easy it would be for me to fall in love with him. I pulled away, but Jacob held me tight and pulled me back in to him.

"I didn't mean to frighten you. I just wanted you to know how I feel about you," he said.

We were barely moving to the music, and Jacob tilted his head back to look at me. At first, I kept my eyes down, and then somehow found the courage to look up into his, and that's when he kissed me. Not a long kiss, but a soft, gentle one that covered my lips, and I was unable to fight the eager response to the touch of his lips.

I hid my face in his shoulder, and didn't want the music to end. But it did, and we made our way back to our table. It was hard for me to keep a hundred thoughts from running through my mind, all of them having to do with being with someone other than my husband.

I was on pins and needles throughout the rest of our dinner, and it was only when Jacob reached for my hand that I was able to relax a little. We danced a few more times, and I was oblivious to others on the floor; it seemed the entire world was in love. And each time Jacob held me in his arms, any fears or doubts about what was going to happen that night dashed from my mind.

At midnight, we stood there on the dance floor along with everyone else. We counted down to midnight, but I could see no one but Jacob there in front of me. He kissed me tentatively at first, like testing the waters, and then I returned his kiss, leaving him with no doubt that I was ready to take that next step.

I knew I didn't need to account to my mother for my budding relationship with Jacob, but as we pulled into our drive, all at once, I felt like a young girl doing something her parents would disapprove of. Suddenly, my confidence wavered and my stomach flipped. There would be no denying Jacob had spent the night with me, and yet I wasn't foolish enough to think she wasn't aware of our relationship.

"My mother told me to have a good time this evening," I said, hesitantly, "but I'm not sure she meant this."

Jacob said, "I could always stay in the other cabin."

I'd felt so sure and confident about my life up here in the mountains; these feelings of doubt were unusual for me. But when I looked at him, the wishful smile in his eyes and his infectious grin made me relax.

"You'll do no such thing," I said.

CHAPTER THIRTY

Here I was, only in my mid-forties, and I'd slept with three men; all of them different, and two by my choice. With all three, I'd felt self-conscious, nervous, and embarrassed to be seen without my clothes on, for I'd been raised to be modest and follow the rules. Even Mr. Fletcher had never seen me completely naked. With Jack, while I never paraded around without clothes, I eventually grew more comfortable. And now I knew I'd do so again with Jacob.

Mabelthree wasn't at all sure what was going on that first night we spent together, and I eventually had to lock her out of the bedroom. Being intimate with Jacob was not complicated; I knew what to do to please him, and with a few tries, he figured me out as well.

The next morning, New Year's Day, I made pancakes and bacon, and we both sat at the table with our coffee. I worried that my mother would stop in, but I also knew that when she saw Jacob's truck still in the drive, she would assume we'd been together.

We spent the rest of the day like an old married couple; Jacob watched football, and I sat next to him on the couch reading. Mabelthree sat at our feet, occasionally looking up at both of us to see what we were doing. She would have to get used to having Jacob around more.

Soon, winter started warming into spring, and Jacob gave up the cabin he rented near the boatyard so he could stay with me on the days he worked in the shop.

"Jacob's a good man," my mother said one day.

"He is. I feel like I'm very fortunate to have found him."

"Do you think you'll ever get remarried?" she asked.

"Oh, I don't know. We've talked about it a little, just comments or thoughts," I said. I knew, as an unmarried couple, it could be considered living in sin, but I never felt anyone we knew treated us any differently than if we were married. "I'm actually happy the way things are for now. I have the cabins and the bookshop and Jacob still needs to be in Big Bear a couple of days a week."

That's where Jacob was for the next two days so my mother and I started putting leftovers together for dinner.

"I wish you would have found someone after my father died," I finally said.

My mother sighed. "I used to think about it, but if I'm honest, I always worried I'd end up with the same kind of man. They say history repeats itself, and anyway, living in the mansion sort of took all of my time."

"Well, it's not too late, you know."

"If truth be told, I've met several men working at the resort. Just none of them suited me. I wouldn't mind the companionship every now and then, though," she said thoughtfully. "In the meantime, I'm up for a promotion."

"You are? Why didn't you say something about it earlier?"

"I didn't want to jinx it. The housekeeping director is retiring, and they want me to take the position." She raised her head in an exaggerated boast.

I hadn't ever seen my mother so animated. She was obviously proud of her achievement. And I was too.

"This calls for a celebration," I said. "Let's go somewhere for dinner. How about we try the new little Italian restaurant? Jacob and I've been there, and it was good."

The air had turned so cold it felt like ice, and I wondered if it might snow. We bundled up in our heavy coats, and we could see clouds of white air on our breath as we walked to the car. I turned the heater on high the minute we got in. We finally warmed up as we pulled into the parking lot, and even though it was warm in the restaurant, we waited until we were seated before we hung our coats on the wall hooks.

There was no snow that night, but the temperature went down to thirty degrees and the next morning, ice covered the ground. I wanted to go in to the bookshop, for I'd received a large shipment of new books from the distributor the day before; Truman Capote's *Breakfast at Tiffany's*, and *The Guinness Book of World Records*, to name a few, and I wanted to get them unpacked. I had called a few of my best customers to let them know they'd arrived and I wanted to have displays set up before we opened.

There were no cars on the roads into the Village, and the quiet almost felt dreamlike, but more of an unearthly than a peaceful dream. Fog was drifting in and everything was gray; the sky, the trees, the cars still parked in driveways. I hadn't recalled ever having that sensation.

There were very few cars in the designated parking lot, and even though it was early, I wondered if businesses were going to open their shops. I pulled my coat tighter as I made my way to the bookshop, and I quickly checked the temperature on the thermostat. It was continually set at fifty degrees to keep the pipes from freezing, but it felt much colder so I turned it up.

I put on a pot of coffee to warm not only me, but for any truly devoted customers who came in throughout the day. I feared only brave souls would be out in this cold. The shop eventually warmed up enough, and I had my displays set up when I looked outside. The village was completely engulfed in fog, and suddenly the store felt airless and enclosed.

"Don't be silly," I told myself, but I still had a difficult time concentration on my bookkeeping.

By noon, I hadn't had a single customer, and my instinct was that no one was going to go out in this weather, so I turned the heater back down and closed up the shop. I inched my way home, and no matter how many times I'd driven in the mountain fog, it always made me nervous. When I finally made it to our drive, my neck muscles were so tight, I had a headache. Thankfully, it was my mother's day off, so I knew she was safe, but I wondered how Jacob was doing with this weather. Was Big Bear experiencing the same cold?

Mabelthree rushed outside like she always did the minute I opened the door, and after only a few minutes, the fog had dampened her coat, and she shook herself before I could get to her with a towel. Her paws were freezing, so I wiped them dry.

I made a call to Jacob's shop, but there was no answer. I figured he was outside bringing in any boats or equipment, but when I tried again and he didn't answer, I began to worry. I knew he'd call me when he had a chance, so I grabbed a couple of blankets and sat on the couch to watch the news.

When I couldn't find a station talking about the weather, I checked with the National Weather Service and they were warning of severe weather and record snowfall heading our way. Finally, Jacob called and confirmed he'd been busy getting everything inside in anticipation of the storm.

"We're in for a doozy," he said, breathing hard. "They're predicting a storm worse than back in the 1930s when snow was six feet high. I wish I was there to help you get ready," he said, "but I'm thinking once it starts snowing, there won't be any way out of here. I don't want to scare you, but you need to make sure you and your mother have plenty of food in the cabin."

"It's so foggy here now, I'm afraid to go out," I said. "I think we have enough."

"Well, bring in plenty of firewood, if you can. Maybe call Robbie to come over in the morning. He's used to driving those roads. You can make a list for him and he can go to the store for you."

"Be careful, Jacob," I said. "I don't have to go out in it."

"I will. And if it gets as bad as they say it will, I don't plan on going anywhere either."

"Call me in the morning," I said.

"I will. Love you."

"Love you too."

Robbie didn't answer his phone, so I put on my heavy jacket and work gloves and started bringing in firewood. I knew black widow spiders made their home in the woodpiles, so I tossed the logs one by one onto the ground to dislodge any that might be hiding in there. I constantly checked to make sure there were none that needed killing before I brought the logs in.

For two days, the snow fell nonstop. More than once, I shoveled out a path to my mother's cabin in case of an emergency. Fearing I'd never be able to keep up with the storm, we gathered some of her clothing and any food she had stored and made our way back down to my cabin.

We heard the constant movement of snowplows that cleared the road in front but they pushed the snow toward us, making it impossible for us to leave the property even if we wanted to. By the time a vehicle could pass on the road, the berm to our driveway was four feet high. The snow didn't stop.

Three days later, when the snow finally stopped, the snow was so high we couldn't see out our windows to the road. Our vehicles were buried, and the only light of day was from the ten feet I'd been able to keep clear out the front of the office. When I looked out the glass in the front door, I felt like I was looking into a road to nowhere. And that's exactly what it was. A road that stopped at a snow wall. At least that small path gave us some daylight and Mabelthree a place to do her business.

I kept the blinds closed, which made the office and cabin dark, but when I opened them to a wall of solid snow, I felt so confined and anxious I paced the floor. I preferred the darkness. It was the deafening silence, though, that was almost unbearable.

Thankfully, we hadn't lost power, and we were able to stay warm. The television was constantly on, the sound sometimes almost vibrating off the wood log walls. The news was filled with stories of the freak storm, and we could hear the small planes periodically flying overhead. They were the only source of images, since no vehicles could get through some of the roads to the people stranded in their homes.

My mother worked on her knitting and I read, but the days dragged on to where they felt like they were a hundred hours long and not twelve. Mabelthree also sensed the tension, for she'd repeatedly scratch at the front door, only to stare into walls of snow when I got up to let her out.

Jacob called regularly; Big Bear was also snowed in but he said there were snowplows running day and night and they were keeping the roads cleared.

"We usually get more snow than Arrowhead, but from the looks of it, you guys are really socked in. We have more equipment and manpower than you do down there," he said. "From what I see on the news, the county needs to bring in more emergency crews."

"I don't care how they do it," I said, "but this is making me stir-crazy. I can only imagine people needing medical help. Someone's going to have to dig the snow away from the buildings. I can't shovel it any higher and some of it's turned to ice."

"Hang in there. I'll get down there as soon as I can and lend a hand. The snowplow is in front of the house now, so I need to go. Just be careful," he said.

"You too."

Later that afternoon, new helicopter images of the town were on the television. When one flew over the large market in town, it took me a moment to recognize what we were looking at; the entire roof of the store had collapsed, leaving only the four perimeter walls standing.

"Oh my god," I said to my mother. "I've never seen anything like this before. Everything is under that roof and in the snow."

I couldn't help but think of Mr. Weatherby, the grocer in town, and wondered if his store was damaged. A lot of town folk did their weekly shopping at the big markets, but they relied on him for a lot of food and staples. In the early fifties, two major supermarkets broke ground at opposite ends of town, and every time I'd go in to pick something up from him, poor Mr. Weatherby was wringing his hands, worrying about what was going to happen to him.

"I don't know whether to pack up and move, or what," he finally said to me one time.

I'd been thinking about his situation, and told him my thoughts.

"You know everyone in town wants to support you, but they'll still need a big store to buy all their meat and paper goods. They'll now stay up here and not go down the mountain. What if you stopped trying to compete with the big guys, and focused on having things we need but don't want to go to the store for? Like milk, bread, soda pop, ice cream, then fill the rest of the store with hardware and small things we hate going to the lumberyard for. Like the store in Cedar Glen, but with groceries. You could become a store for convenience."

"Hmm. You might have an idea there," he said, scratching his chin. "I could sell plungers, some small tools for fixin' things around the house. Drain cleaner—why I think you've just saved my business, Ruth."

"Well, it goes to show you it helps to talk to people, doesn't it? Start asking people what they'd like to see you carry."

"Here," he said, handing me my bag. "Your groceries are on me today."

"Thanks," I said. "Glad I could help."

That day, I walked out of there feeling like a million bucks. But right now, I wondered how his store had fared. From what I could see on the television, it looked like everything in town was still buried. A newscaster was telling people that if they had a medical emergency, to call the number on the screen, and somehow, crews would try to get them out. It sounded logical, but I wasn't sure how they'd be able to identify any of the houses if people couldn't get outside to mark where they were. What if people died because they couldn't get out?

CHAPTER THIRTY ONE

Just thinking about all the terrible things that could be happening made my stomach churn. If I wasn't on edge by the bleak silence, I was exhausted. Once, when I lay down to take a nap just as I dozed off, Mabelthree jumped on the bed and nudged me. Her whine was faint, but she either wanted to go outside or was hungry. I opened the front door first, but she didn't budge, so I brought out her dog food bag and by the weight of it I could tell we were running low.

"Sorry, girl," I said as I tore up some bread and added it and water to a few bites of dry food. "Don't inhale your food. We need to make it last."

On the fourth day, Jacob called and said he was heading over. He wasn't sure what he'd be able to do, but if he couldn't get close to the cabins, he'd see where the crews could use him. Later that morning, I heard a snowplow on the road, and when it stopped at our property, I hoped beyond hope it would stay to begin digging us out. When it drove on, my heart sank. I turned the television back on, and an announcer who had a camera on the highway said, "We're starting to see some relief. The county is getting a lot of criticism for not sending more crews in sooner."

The next morning, I heard the snowplow again, and then I heard the crunching of snow near us as it carved out its first load. The question was, where was all that snow going to go? By early afternoon, the last few feet of snow were being hauled off the drive, and three men were digging a path to the office. Suddenly, Jacob came in to view and my heart leapt. The feeling of impending doom was being lifted.

"Mother, he's here," I called out. I opened the front door and shouted, "Watch for the dog poop—" but not before Jacob stepped right into it.

"Shit!" he cried out. "At least she had a place to go."

"You must be freezing," I said, bringing him some paper towels to wipe his boots.

Within the hour, we were free. I hadn't realized how much I'd missed seeing the ground. My car was still buried, but once I could get Robbie out here, he could help Jacob dig it out.

I called Mr. Weatherby at the store to make sure everything was all right, and thankfully, he was open. I'd made a list of things I needed and he said, "I've got Robbie making deliveries for me if you can't get in."

"I'll have Jacob make a trip in, but thanks," I said.

"This whole thing's just a mess, isn't it?" he said. "He'll see when he gets here. He'll have to walk through about an eight-foot high passageway just to get to the store."

My mother and I spent the day cleaning the cabin and doing laundry, but all the while, I couldn't keep from worrying about the bookshop. If that roof caved in, I would be out of business, not to mention losing some irreplaceable books. Robbie was in high demand with Mr. Weatherby's deliveries and said it would probably be a week before he could get over to help dig my car out. I told him not to worry; we had Jacob's truck, so at least we could get around if we had to.

Jacob shoveled a fresh path to my mother's cabin. The snow was still about six feet deep in places and it felt like walking through an ice tunnel, but at least she could now stay in her own home. It took almost another week to get the local businesses along the main roads up and running. When Jacob drove me over to the Village, they'd finally plowed the entrance and parking lot enough that we could drive in. We watched as two plows alternated dropping full loads of snow into the lake. They cleared the square in front of the small businesses enough for us to dig pathways to our shops. I'd dreaded finding out how the Village had fared, and I was more than relieved there'd been no damage to the buildings or roofs. My books were safe.

The next day, we heard the highway was closed due to a landslide. Traffic was at a standstill for another week while workers cleared the road. The after effects of the storm had created a nightmare for everyone. Visitors and residents were stranded; no one could get up and down the mountain, and businesses were still closed, some most likely even permanently.

I knew most of the townspeople weren't ready to get out and shop for books, but I opened anyway for a change of scenery. Jacob left me in the store while he drove over to the boatyard. When he came to pick me up, he told me that other than some buried equipment, everything was intact. There hadn't been as much snow there as everywhere else, and icicles were melting off his roof.

We grabbed a quick lunch and headed back to the cabin. I'd missed Jacob in more ways than one and the moment we closed the door behind us, I playfully kissed him long and arduously. He took that as his sign to lay me down on my bed.

"I feel kind of weird doing this in the daylight," I said.

"There's always a time to try something new," he said, enveloping me in his kisses.

Once the snow melted enough, like everyone else, I fought my way through the grocery store that was still standing. Monitors were on every aisle to make sure people didn't hoard paper products and food. At the checkout counter, the cashier made customers set aside anything over the store limit. I recognized more than one family split up their shopping, even going to different check stands hoping no one would notice what they were doing.

While there were few guests at the resort, as head of housekeeping, my mother had to report back to work. There was a lot to do to get the hotel back up and running.

Within two weeks, the mountain residents were eager to get back to some sort of normalcy, and even with mounds of snow around us, we were grateful for what we had. Once the snow melted off the roofs and we could shovel snow away from the cabins, I sighed in relief to confirm we'd had no damage.

The newspaper ran an article about three deaths; Randall Moore of Crestline missed his dialysis and died of kidney failure, and Mabel Green and Walter Watson, both from Lake Arrowhead, died of heart attacks. I couldn't help but think how frightened those people must have been, knowing they couldn't get help when they so desperately needed it.

On the positive side, visitors were coming back up the mountain to see what was going on and we had a few bookings at the cabins. The bookshop was busy, and Jacob was back in Big Bear at the other boat shop.

And my mother met a man.

CHAPTER THIRTY TWO

His name was Ray Johnson. He'd been a volunteer helping the crews on our property during the storm, and that's when they met. For the first time in years, I saw a spark return to my mother's eyes when she talked about him. His wife died a long time ago, and he lived up in the mountains on his own. I met him when his three children, who lived in different parts of the country, came up to celebrate his 70th birthday.

It was clear when I saw them together, he had strong feelings for my mother and I realized a piece of her life had been put back together. He had an easy smile, and when my mother spoke, he focused only on her and what she was saying. He told silly jokes, which made her laugh, and often when they walked together, he took her hand. More than once, I wondered what it would have been like to have a father who was so kind and caring.

After March's terrible snowstorm, I never would have imagined the ferns would have come back so fully, but they grew everywhere. Tulips and daffodils popped up, and the dogwoods bloomed in abundance.

"Always remember," my mother said. "After every winter comes spring."

That summer, a wedding party booked six of our cabins. It was both unusual and a little nerve-wracking to have such a large party, and I left the bookshop early to get everyone settled in. When the bride and groom checked in, I suddenly felt old. It wasn't just their youth; it was their un-abashed love for each other that struck me. Maybe I was just turning in to a hopeless romantic, for I watched the way she touched his arm as he signed the register, the way he pulled her toward him in a quick hug, and the kiss to her forehead as they waited for me to finish my paperwork.

"Which cabin would you like to spend your honeymoon in?" I asked.

"We don't care," the groom-to-be said, and they both giggled.

"Ah, to be young again," I said, and they giggled again. "Let me know, for I'll have a little surprise waiting for you."

"My cabin," the bride said. "Let's stay in mine, since all my things will already be in there."

It was late in the afternoon when I put a bottle of champagne in the refrigerator to chill. I found the bucket in the pantry and had just started shining it up when I heard a car pull in to the lot. A few minutes later, a man stood in the doorway to the office. His disheveled hair was wild and dried blood had run from his nose to around his mouth. At first, I thought he'd been in a fight, and when I held my hand to my *own* face and asked him if he was all right, he instinctively raised his hand to his nose and lips. When he pulled it away, it surprised him to find blood.

"I swerved to miss a deer," was all he said.

I studied him for a minute and didn't feel any fear; he was scattered, but I thought it was because of his near accident.

"Do you need help?" I asked.

"I'm looking for a place to stay," he said flatly.

"How long will you be staying?" I asked, opening our guest book.

"Oh, tonight," he said, looking around the office. "Maybe tomorrow night, too. I'll pay you for both now."

He hadn't moved from the doorway, and I began to wonder if he was all right. I should have felt apprehension, but I didn't. Instead, I felt consolation and compassion for him. He was obviously in shock.

"Here you go," I said. "You're in cabin number five. Would you like me to show you how to light the fireplace in case you get chilly? Even in summer, it can cool down quite a bit."

"No. I'm good. I can figure it out. I doubt I'll get cold," he said.

"John Murphy?" I asked, turning the guest book around to read it.

"Thanks," he said as he turned and left.

I chewed the inside of my cheek, then shrugged my shoulders. It would have been terrible if he'd hit that deer, or even killed himself trying to avoid it.

The next morning, John Murphy's car was gone, so I assumed he was all right. I let Mabelthree out, then changed the hours on the clock sign. When I got home, John Murphy's car was back in the parking lot, so I presumed he was going to stay the second night. It was still there in the morning when I left for the bookshop and I never gave it another thought until I got home that afternoon to find it still there.

There was no note on the door letting me know he wanted to stay another night, so I went down and knocked on the door. There was no answer, so I figured he was either in the shower or out for a walk. I didn't have bookings that day, so I didn't worry about him being there the extra morning. Maria Lopez, who was a housekeeper at the Resort helped me clean the cabins when someone checked out. When I got to the bookshop, I called her to see if she could go by and clean number five that afternoon after work. We didn't have another booking for the cabin so it wouldn't matter what time she cleaned it.

I had a busy day; a shipment of books came in from the distributor; James A. Michener's *Hawaii*, and Ian Fleming's *Goldfinger* among them. I moved last month's books to another table and arranged the newest books into stacks and onto easels and set out more bookmarks. Our 'New Books' sign was beginning to look ratty, so I called the printer to make me up another one.

At three-thirty, I answered the phone, and it was Maria.

"He's dead!" she cried.

"Who is?" My heart was racing.

"The man! He's dead! He didn't answer when I knocked on the door, so I opened the door."

"Don't go in there! I'll call the sheriff!"

"I knew it," I said aloud as I dialed the operator. Mr. Murphy probably died from his head injury. I should have done a more thorough job of checking on him. When the operator came on, my hands were shaking and my voice cracked. I gave her the address of the cabins, and then locked up the bookshop and headed for home.

When I got to the cabins, there was barely enough room for me to pull into the driveway. The flashing lights of the sheriff's car caught in the sunlight, and I wished he'd turn them off. An ambulance parked off to the right, its rear doors open and an empty gurney sat outside. The sheriff was attempting to console Maria, who was frantically wiping her eyes.

"What's happened?" I asked as I rushed over.

"You can't go in there, Ruth," Sheriff Griffin said, holding his arm out to block me. "He's hung himself."

"Dear god," was all I could say.

"What was his name?"

"John Murphy,"

Early the next afternoon, the crime scene tape came down, and they towed John Murphy's car away. Robbie and Jacob spent the rest of the afternoon taking the bed apart and moving all the furniture to one side of the room.

"Burn all the linens and take the mattress to the dump," I said. I couldn't touch them and there was no way I was going to let guests stay there again.

Robbie let it slip that not all of the hanging rope was removed, and part of it was still tied around the rafter. He climbed up there and cut it down. We locked the door to that cabin and I never went in there again. Over the next year, Jacob and Robbie were the only ones who would go in, and it ended up becoming a store-all. When we did any work in the rest of the cabins, if something was worth keeping, like old light fixtures or plumbing parts, it went into cabin five. We filled it with old mattresses in case we needed them in an emergency, roll-away beds, and old furniture that had gotten broken but was too good to throw away.

When I replaced bed linens and curtains in one of the cabins, the old ones went into a large plastic bag and we stored them, too. Everything we didn't know what to do with, including boxes of old files and a desk chair, went in to cabin number five.

With everyone traipsing all over the ground, the gravel was either strewn about or pressed into the ground, and the flowers in front of cabin five were trampled. I went to the small nursery In town, bought a few containers of flowers, and I thought I wouldn't have a problem replanting them. But when I brought them back, all I could do was stand there. It was as if the boogie man was going to get me if I got too near the cabin. I ended up asking Robbie to plant them for me and replace a layer of gravel.

I'd never seen John Murphy hanging there, but images of him played over and over in my mind, and sometimes I couldn't sleep because those visions were so clear. Even Mabelthree sensed something was wrong in the cabin. For months after John Murphy's death, when we let her out, she'd run to cabin five and whine. It made the hair on the back of my neck stand on end.

Maria ended up leaving the mountain, and I had to say I didn't blame her. She never went back to work at the resort; she simply disappeared, and no one heard from her again. The newspaper ran a few stories about John Murphy's death, and the mystery behind it, but eventually nothing else was written. It was just as well. I didn't want to think about it anymore than I already did.

CHAPTER THIRTY THREE

Time seems to have a way of making bad memories fade, and that was true when, in 1959, Jacob asked me to marry him.

"What will I do with the bookshop?" I asked.

"Open one in Big Bear."

He still had his two boat shops, so when I suggested we keep the bookshop in the Village and come in the same days he came in now, it seemed like a perfect solution if Julie could work full time. But then I thought about the biggest move, and that would be to leave the cabins.

"What would I do?" I asked him.

"If you sell them, you could tuck away the money, or you could use it to open the second store."

Jacob's house in Big Bear would be a comfortable place for us to stay if I changed a few things. The first opportunity we had, we stayed there a few days and I shared with him my ideas. There was room for my sewing machine, pots and pans, and the hope chest that Dorothy never took. I needed bookcases for all my books and I found the perfect spot for the ones Jack had built me. When I asked Jacob how he'd feel if I brought them along, he was fine with the idea. I liked the oil painting over the fireplace in the lobby, so we brought that over also. I wasn't much of a frilly person, but I wanted to brighten up the place with new rugs and curtains for all the rooms. He agreed, and we made a trip down to the

Sears store in San Bernardino and bought everything I'd asked for, including a new bed. If we were going to start a new life together, I wanted where we slept to be new to both of us.

When I told my mother about my plans with Jacob, she wasn't surprised.

"Ray has asked if I would consider being with him," she said.

"*Mother*," I said, surprised. "Do you know him well enough?"

"You know, Ruth, I've never said anything about you and Jacob." I could tell she was a little miffed. "And Ray and I aren't getting any younger. I'll be sixty-five this year and I'd like to be happy before I die."

"I'm sorry," I said, reaching for her arm. "I never meant it to come out that way." Suddenly, tears filled my eyes. "I want nothing more than for you to be happy. You deserve that more than anyone. I wish you would have found him years ago—you obviously just caught me by surprise."

"And I didn't mean to snap at you, Ruth. I think I could be happy with him, and for the first time, I want to give it a try."

"If I sell the cabins, will you go stay with him?"

"Yes. I know it'll be frowned upon for someone my age, but I don't really care what people think."

"Then good for you. Actually, I'm really happy for you and relieved you'll be safe without me."

"I'll be fine, Ruth. Don't worry about me. You've given me a wonderful life here and we both deserve a new start, don't we?"

The Friday night before our wedding, my mother, Ray, Jacob and I had dinner at the Italian restaurant Jacob liked. We toasted to each other and to our new journeys. On Saturday morning, Jack Jr. and Dorothy came up with their families and stayed in the cabins.

There was a small chapel where a lot of couples came up to get married. It overlooked the rim and on most days, thick beautiful white clouds that made you feel like you could walk out on to covered the view of the valley below and came up to the mountain. On our wedding day, my wish for those clouds came true, and when we looked out, it was almost like we were in heaven.

After the wedding, we all had dinner at the Resort. My mother had the baker make us a beautiful one layer cake, covered in wisps of clouds, pine trees and little hearts. And on Sunday, Jacob and I headed down the hill for our honeymoon.

On the highway down the mountain, when the old white hotel came in to view, I thought about how I came to live up in the mountains. I'd told Jacob I'd worked for a wealthy family in Seattle, but only that I didn't want that kind of life anymore. I knew if I didn't tell him now, he would feel I'd betrayed him by me not telling him about an important part of my life. It'd been so long ago, and strangely, I felt it was something that'd happened to someone else. I was not that person anymore, and even before Dorothy was born, Jack and I felt it was best if she grew up knowing *him* as her father.

Jacob and I headed down to Palm Springs for our honeymoon. In the few minutes it took us to pass the now abandoned hotel, I struggled with myself whether to tell Jacob about my past; and as I'd done so many other times we passed it, I decided some things were better left untold.

I'd never been to the desert before, and once we got close, I realized I wasn't a fan of the red soil and parched looking landscape. I preferred the green of the mountains. Our hotel was right on the main drive into town, and other than the hotel I stayed in with the Fletchers so many years ago, I realized I hadn't stayed in one since.

As we drove up to the entrance, a valet took our name and unloaded our luggage. A bellman took our suitcases and led us into the lobby, where several couples ahead of us were checking in. I couldn't help but notice the bellman waiting to take us up to our room, and once we got off the elevator, we passed maids finishing up several rooms ahead of us. The bellman brought our luggage in and waited for Jacob's tip, then bowed and said thank you.

"Enjoy your stay," he said. "Oh, I almost forgot, here's a map to the homes of the old movie stars, if you're interested."

"Did you know that beginning in the 1930s, Palm Springs was an oasis for movie stars such as Bob Hope, Edward G. Robinson and aviator/film producer Howard Hughes?" I asked Jacob as I read the map. "Can we drive around tomorrow?"

"I don't see why not," Jacob answered, unpacking our suitcases. "Do you want to just eat in the hotel tonight?"

I flipped through the guest directory and said, "We can either have the coffee shop, steak or Italian," I said. "Steak sounds good to me; I'll make a reservation, but first, I'd love to take a quick nap."

We had time to spare before dinner, so we walked around the hotel and ended up outside by the pool. The weather was nice enough to sit at one of the tables and although it was growing dark out, several people were still swimming.

"I don't think I even have a swimsuit," I said. "Plus, I wouldn't want everyone looking at me."

"You let me look at you," Jacob said, taking my hand and bringing it to his lips.

"That's barely."

"You look good, Ruth."

"But I don't look like those girls."

"Do you want to be those girls? Look at everything you have."

"When you put it that way," I crooked my smile, "no."

"See."

Jacob looked at his watch and got up. "Let's go eat."

Dinner was delicious, and I could tell Jacob was getting eager to get back to our room. It wasn't as though it was the first night we'd slept together, but it was the first one as husband and wife. I was feeling a little jittery, and I wanted to relax and take a nice warm bath. Jacob took his shower while I brushed out my hair and wound it up in a knot.

I lay in the warm water, my insides jangling with expectation, and my heart swelled just thinking about how lucky I was to have another chance to fill my life with love. I wanted the evening to be perfect.

"We're going to turn into pumpkins!" Jacob playfully called out.

"Just a sec."

I wrapped my hair loosely in a towel, then draped my body in a second one. I came into our room and Jacob had turned off all the lights except for a floor lamp off to one side.

"Tada!" I said, dropping first the towel that covered my body, then the one that released my hair.

Our bodies were in harmony with each other, and contentment flowed between us.

CHAPTER THIRTY FOUR

A month later, the cabins officially went up for sale; I put a For Sale sign out on the highway and talked with a real estate person about handling the sale when someone was interested. Jacob stayed there with me when he was in town. The plan was that when I sold them, we'd look for a small cabin in Cedar Glen near the boat shop. I was so filled with emotions; one part of me wanted to sell the cabins and move on; I was ready for a new adventure both in Big Bear and wherever we found our new home. But part of me was worried about leaving the book shop even though Julie would be a perfect manager. I was also growing impatient to find or open a new store in Big Bear. My mood changed every day.

I'd been to Ray's house before, but my mother and I went there one morning to look at it from a different point of view, and we made a list of a few things she wanted to do. Like Jacob's house, it needed curtains, new towels, and new bedding, so we made a trip down to the Sears store, then went to the soda fountain and had lunch and a malt. A week later, she moved in, and I had to admit it felt like one of my children had moved away from home again.

I knew she wasn't going to be that far away, but it was as if I'd lost a part of me. When I looked outside now, it was strange to see that her cabin was dark. There was an empty space where her car was no longer parked, and I had no one to share an evening of television with if Jacob was in Big Bear. I phoned her every day for the first few days, just to make sure she was all right. I made up some silly reason for the call, but it was really out of selfishness on my part.

A few people came to look at the cabins and said they'd get back in touch with me if they were interested. And one afternoon, a husband and wife came up and even before they said they were interested, I knew they were the ones.

Sam and Trudy Jackson were from down in San Diego, and both were retiring early from teaching. They'd looked at several places in Big Bear, but when they saw how quaint Lake Arrowhead was, they decided this was where they wanted to move. Like me when I moved up, they were totally unfamiliar with mountain life, but also like me, and the many others before us, they'd figure it out.

"Where can we get a bite to eat and talk about it?" Sam asked. "We can come back and let you know either way."

I gave them directions to the coffee shop in town and told them I'd be here when they got back. I immediately called Jacob and told him I'd just met the perfect couple, and I just knew they were going to buy the cabins.

"I just have a feeling," I said.

I made myself a sandwich and went through last week's newspaper. I was too nervous to eat, but found a couple of houses near Jacob's boat shop. When I called the first one, it had already been rented, and my stomach sank. A little disheartened, I called the second one expecting to hear the same, but the woman on the other end of the phone said, "Yes, it's still available."

"I'll have my husband drive by," I said.

Then I called Jacob back and gave him the address. He said he'd take a quick break and go by it.

Forty-five days later, Sam and Trudy Jackson were the new owners of the cabins. On the Saturday after it closed escrow, I drove through the town with a new perspective; I'd shared my plans with the store owners where I shopped, but on this day, I said a form of 'goodbye'. I'd be back once a week with Jacob, and work at the bookshop, but it wasn't going to be the same. I wouldn't see these people every day, and I'd most likely find new places to shop in Big Bear. I felt both saddened, and light-hearted thinking about my future.

The Sunday after we closed escrow, I spent the day with the Jacksons, going over everything about running the cabins. On Monday, I officially moved out of the cabins and into my new life with Jacob. And on Tuesday, they moved in.

A little over six months later, I began looking in earnest for a place to open another book shop in Big Bear. The one bookshop in town was in a smaller, older building just outside the main shopping district. It smelled old and musty, and I knew even if I took it over, it wouldn't be large enough to carry enough new books. Plus even if I took everything out and replaced the carpet, I'd never get that old smell out of the place. Big Bear was much different from Lake Arrowhead; the community was larger, it had a true downtown, and there were a lot of shops and restaurants to attract tourists.

I eventually came across an available store in town next to an ice cream shop, and when Jacob saw it, he agreed it would be a perfect location for my bookshop. The front window was large enough for display, and the space itself was a good size for used and new books. By selling the cabins, I had enough money to comfortably open the store, and I could open another savings account as well. I signed the lease, and two months later, we had an open house for Books & Co. II.

Once a week, when I came back in to Lake Arrowhead my mother would bring lunch in from the sandwich shop across the way from the bookshop in the Village, and we'd get caught up on her life with Ray and her work at the resort. She was thinking about retiring, but was worried she wouldn't have anything to do all day.

"All I've done is work," she said.

A yarn and quilting shop opened in the Village, and she joined a knitting club. She constantly made sweaters for her great-grandchildren, and although she could have bought them in the dress shop in town, she knitted us matching caps and scarves.

I found a young woman who made candles and soaps, and we started selling them in both the shops. When I opened the stores each morning, I'd stop and breathe in the muskiness of their fragrance and the old books. A local photographer brought in some greeting cards with his images on them, and we set up a small display near the cash register. I asked if he'd make some with Big Bear on them, and about a week later, he brought some in to the store there. Customers enjoyed picking up little gifts that were unique to the shops.

In all the time I'd lived in Lake Arrowhead, I'd only been to Big Bear a few times, and I didn't know a lot about it. I decided to carry books by local authors who used it as their backdrop and wrote about its history and lore. And when I had a quiet moment or two, I'd read them.

I never knew that like Lake Arrowhead, over two thousand years ago, the Serrano Indians lived there. I learned that a bear hunter discovered gold in the area and it's the winter home to the bald eagle. They say it's one of the sunniest places in the world. And I believe them.

AUTHOR'S NOTES

I began writing The Guest Book Trilogy about Annie and the cabins, but as I finished editing book three, *The Starlet in Cabin Number Seven*, I was curious about the cabins before Annie bought them.

If you've started with *The Maidservant in Cabin Number One*, this is the beginning, or the prequel of what's now become a series.

The Man in Cabin Number Five is the beginning of the Trilogy.

Coming soon, *Dear Noah*, is the Guest Book sequel. It continues Annie's story until she's in her eighties and writes about this time in her life.

I hope I haven't confused you!

As with my other books, I've taken creative liberties to fit actual events into the timeline of my story. Many sets of eyes scanned these pages before printing, but typos still seem to evade me, and I'd love it if you'd let me know if anything jumps out at you. I'll correct it for the next printing.

I want to thank my husband Larry, who has always been so supportive; he's my sounding board when I'm stuck, my encouragement when I wonder about my work, and my cheering section when things go well, and even if they don't.

I'd also like to thank my original first readers, **Myrt Perisho**, **Pat Aldridge** and **Susan Denley**. I trust them to read from a "reader's" point of view; my main question to them is did you like the story and would they read another? **Sue Jorgenson** tries to find most of my typos, and my editor **Pam Sheppard** makes sure my storyline makes sense and is going in the right direction.

Book Clubs: If you're in Southern California, and your book club would like to read any of my books, please let me know. I'd love to come and talk to you! If you're not in my area, I'd still love to hear from you; I have a book bag, bookmarks, notepads and a journal I can send for your meeting.

I've met some wonderful new people on my writing journey and I love hearing from my readers. Email me at chrysteenbraun@gmail.com and let me know if you have any thoughts or comments. I promise. I'll reply.

Check out my website at www.chrysteenbraun.com and subscribe to my newsletter. While you're there, check out my bookmarks and notepad. If you'd like one, just drop me a line with your name and address.

Thanks for reading!

Chrysteen

Interesting Notes, or in other words, going down the proverbial rabbit hole when I'm doing research!

Nashville, Tennessee

When trying to decide where my character, Ruth Landry, came from, I looked at a map of the U.S., and decided Nashville, Tennessee, seemed like a good place to start. I've never been there, and while my research produced only a few lines in the actual story, I discovered the history of the town was interesting to note.

In 1714, French traders established a trading post and settlement at the present location of downtown Nashville, named for Francis Nash, an American Revolutionary war hero. Because of its strategic location, by 1800, the city had over three hundred residents, including about 135 enslaved African Americans and fourteen freedmen. In 1806 Nashville was incorporated and in 1843 it became the capital.

Tennessee was a Confederate state before the Civil War, and over 3,200 enslaved African Americans lived in the city. They helped to build the successful water system and maintained the city's streets. Nashville and Jefferson Street became the center of the African American community and a destination for Jazz and Blues musicians, and eventually, country music.

Tennessee is known for its tobacco plantations and breeding and training thoroughbred horses. It was the first state to fall to Union Troops.

Seattle, Washington

I wanted Ruth Ann and her family to end up on the west coast, so I chose Seattle, Washington, as the next stop for my character.

Built on Indigenous land, where the Suquamish and Duwamish Tribes first lived, forest trees up to 2,000 years old towered upward of 400 feet high, covering much of what is now the city of Seattle.

On June 6, 1889, the Great Seattle Fire burned twenty-nine blocks of wooden buildings, destroying records of banks, stores, doctors offices, lawyers offices and warehouses. The fire started in a basement cabinet shop when a pot of melting glue ignited.

Rebuilding began immediately, and ordinances were quickly passed, requiring new buildings to use only bricks and stone. Many of their first and second stories were below ground, and they lined the alleys with brick walls, which made the new buildings twelve to thirty feet higher than before.

Eventually, these underground levels were abandoned, and are no longer in use; they're Seattle's Underground.

Rodeo Drive, Beverly Hills, California

I created my own timeline for Rodeo Drive, in Beverly Hills, so that Mrs. Fletcher and her sister could go shopping. It wasn't until 1961 that Fred Hayman opened Giorgio, Beverly Hills, the first high-end boutique. Then came Gucci in 1968, Van Cleef & Arpels in 1969, Vidal Sassoon in 1970, and Polo in 1971.

The story of Arrowhead Springs, Lake Arrowhead, California

In 1863, Arrowhead Springs opened as a sanatorium, treating patients with consumption, otherwise known as tuberculosis. Since then, it's had a flame-colored past. In 1885, it burned down, and was rebuilt. In 1895, it was destroyed by fire again. In 1920, it was used as a convalescent hospital for WWI soldiers. In 1938, it burned again and was rebuilt as the current resort hotel, attracting celebrities like Humphrey Bogart, Loretta Young, Spencer Tracy and Bugsy Siegel.

In 1944 it was turned into a naval hospital, and then in 1946, Conrad Hilton purchased the property and Elizabeth Taylor and Nicky Hilton honeymooned there in 1950. In 1961, it was sold to Campus Crusade for Christ, a non-profit, evangelical Christian organization, and when they moved their headquarters to Orlando, Florida, the hotel went up for sale but remained vacant until San Manuel purchased it in 2017.

A Brief History of Lake Arrowhead

For hundreds of years, Paiute and Serrano Indian tribes lived in the mountains and valleys called Little Bear Valley. In the 1920s, it was renamed Lake Arrowhead for the rock and vegetation formation in the shape of an arrowhead on the face of the San Bernardino Mountains.

In 1979, The Village, which was known as the downtown of Lake Arrowhead, was showing its age, so the owners conducted a "Burn to Learn" exercise, which leveled everything but the original Pavilion, the post office and a real estate office. They rebuilt the center in the same Norman style as the original.

The Lake Arrowhead Landmark

Anyone who's driven up Hwy 18 to Lake Arrowhead and its surrounding communities has seen the shape of a large arrowhead on the southern face of the mountain. It's known as the Lake Arrowhead Landmark.

Native Americans had a widespread belief it was a natural feature. A Native American tribe called Guachina believed a white arrow of light struck down on the mountain after they sacrificed their chief's maiden daughter to end a drought. The Heat Spirit, the cause of the drought, drowned and created the bubbling hot water that became the hot springs.

The Cahuilla Tribal legend believed a "flaming arrow of light" embedded itself on to the mountainside, which they took as a sign the valley was the place they would call home.

Spanish explorers referred to the arrowhead in 1810, but others believe there was no mention of the landmark by Spanish inhabitants in the early 1840s. In a photo from 1864, sanatorium founder David Noble Smith poses in front of the original buildings and the arrowhead is clearly visible.

Over the years, conservation groups, including the Boy Scouts, have spent thousands of hours maintaining the site. Soil samples were taken and tested, and in 1998, they determined the soil within the arrowhead differed from the surrounding areas.

The arrowhead has survived several fires from 1885 to 2003.

Boscobel, Wisconsin

I've never been to Boscobel, Wisconsin, but I got the idea of using it as Sam and Trudy's hometown after talking with my daughter's father-in-law who was originally from there. The Boscobel Hotel was originally called the Central House, and it was a saloon until it burned in 1881. After it was rebuilt, and by the time of Mr. Bobel's death, it had become a noted hotel.

I took liberty in bringing the prison to Boscobel in the 1900s, but it was actually built in 1999 as the Supermax Correctional Institution. In 2003, they renamed it the Wisconsin Secure Program Facility.

Big Bear Lake

Like Lake Arrowhead, Big Bear Lake is a man-made lake and dam. In the late 1880s the citrus growers in Redlands hoped the dam would provide them with irrigation water, but it didn't produce sufficient water. In 1912, a new dam was constructed and the Big Bear Municipal Water District acquired the dam in 1977. In 2009 the new bridge was built.

With often over 100 inches of snow each year, Big Bear Lake was a mecca for gold mining before it became a four-season resort. Once known for grizzly bears, by 1906 unregulated hunting killed off the bears. Big Bear has a zoo, a solar observatory, and is known for being one of the sunniest places in the world.

Along with Arrowhead, it also has a rich film history; beginning in 1911 it's been the backdrop for films like *The Last of The Mohicans* with Randolph Scott, *Gone With the Wind,* with Vivien Leigh and Clark Gable, *Old Yeller,* starring Fess Parker and Chuck Connors, and *The Parent Trap* with Hayley Mills, Brian Keith and Maureen O'Hara.

Another interesting note, because of its high elevation (over 7,000 ft.) it's been a popular place for athletes like Oscar De La Hoya and Mike Tyson to train.

Wildhaven Ranch

I've mentioned Wildhaven in all my books, and they continue to be one of my favorite causes. They rescue injured animals and preserve the wildlife. They suffered a lot of damage but thankfully no animals were injured. If you're interested in knowing more about them, check them out at <u>www.wildhavenranch.org</u>. They'd love your support.

Timberline in the Glen, Cedar Glen, California

Truly one of my favorite stores in the mountains, Timberline is, as my friend Cheryl said when she first saw it, "fab.u.lous.!!" They not only have one-of-a-kind wonderful furniture and accessories but every time I go in there, they've redone displays and made the store even more exciting to explore. I found so many incredible and unique pieces there when we were decorating our home in Cedar Ridge Estates.

If you're ever up in Lake Arrowhead, they are a must see.

Oh, and did I mention, they carry my book?

And finally, the snowstorm of all snowstorms in 2023.

While I wrote about a major snowstorm, I got the idea from the March 2023 storm which brought record-breaking snowfall to Lake Arrowhead and surrounding communities, with an estimated 9 feet of snow falling over the course of just a few days. This snowstorm was one of the worst in the area's history, leading to road closures, extensive damage to buildings, power outages, landslides and even death to some who were trapped in their homes for days and could not seek medical care.

County services weren't prepared for such a storm and the damage it caused. Those who weren't snowbound checked on their neighbors and unfortunately several people died because they couldn't get medical care. We have pilot friends who were very instrumental in getting food and pet supplies brought up and air lifted into the community. And because of the generosity of volunteers, a lot of people were able to get the help they needed.

We have friends and family and even a few readers, who suffered property damage but thankfully no injury, and for that, we are all grateful.

Keep reading for a sneak peek at
Dear Noah: The Conclusion

Part One

Noah

NOAH

You might wonder how, after so many years, I can still recall the first time I laid eyes on Annie Parker. It was a Monday, and I was on my way back from the lumberyard when I stopped to check in on Sam. He'd been like a second father to me after my parents died, and now it was my turn to look after him. The door to one of the cabins was open and I could tell by the extra car in the drive that he had a guest.

The air was so still, my boots crunching on the gravel echoed as I made my way down there.

"Hey, Sam," I said, leaning on the doorjamb.

A suitcase was sitting on the bed, and Sam and a young woman turned to look in my direction. My heart turned over and I couldn't take my eyes off her. In that split second, I took in her large dark eyes and her pouty mouth. There was something about her that drew me in. Tight jeans and a red knit sweater completed the picture—and I lost my train of thought.

"Oh, Annie," Sam said. "This is Noah Chambers. He's a local, and since my wife died, he seems to think he has to check in on me."

"I heard that," I said.

Sam shook his head but chuckled. He then opened a cupboard, took out some towels and set them on the bed. "But I do appreciate it," he whispered with a crinkled smile.

They both stood there as if waiting for me to say something else, but it was hard for me to focus on what to say next. What I wanted to say was, 'I can't believe you're so incredibly beautiful.' But the woman turned her head back to her task at hand—unlocking her suitcase—and I lost my opportunity to say something profound.

She grabbed the towels and turned toward the bathroom, and Sam just stared at me. He raised his eyebrows, and I knew he could read my mind. When I saw it was obvious she wasn't going to talk to me, I dumbly said to Sam, "Well, it looks like you're in good hands for now, so I'll get back to work. Nice to meet you, Annie," I called out.

She either didn't hear me, or just wasn't in a friendly mood. I turned and headed back to my truck, listening again to my boots on the gravel, the sound roaring in my head.

All the way back to the job site, I couldn't help but think about her; the way her long dark hair fell onto her face when she bent over, and then how she brushed it back with her hand. And those eyes. I couldn't put my finger on it, but they were so out of the ordinary— almost seductive.

I knew I was going to have to figure out who she was, and then my mind went into overload as I wondered how I'd see her again, much less find out if she was interested in me. Even though I knew it probably wouldn't go anywhere, I had a hard time trying to focus on my work.

At around one, my stomach started growling, and I was at a good stopping point to grab a bite for lunch. I hadn't been to the Sports Grill for a while, so after my guys said they wanted to stay on the job and work, I drove into town by myself. Because I was on my own, I planned to eat at the bar. I walked in and let my eyes acclimate for a few seconds, and when I looked to my right, Annie Parker was sitting by herself at a table watching one of the televisions.

My plan to eat at the bar changed, and I cleared my throat as I walked over to her table.

"Hey, there," I said.

Boy, did she give me a look. I almost said to myself, forget it, but instead, I raised my hands in mock surrender and said, "Hey, I'm Noah. I met you at the cabins, with Sam."

She looked down at my work boots, and her demeanor completely changed. Her face softened and something like a smile surfaced.

"The sun was in my eyes, so I didn't get a good look at your face," she said. "But I recognize your boots."

"Mind if I join you?" I asked.

"Sure."

I sat across from her.

"Are you by yourself?" I asked, and then realized how dumb that sounded—she was by herself when she checked into the cabins.

"Yes, I am," she said.

"Where are you from?"

"Long Beach."

"I'm originally from up here. Never did like it down the hill. How long are you up for?"

She sighed. "A week, or maybe two. Depending on how I feel. I'd forgotten how beautiful it is here, and I need a break."

Suddenly, her dark eyes took on a sad look, and I was curious to know more about her.

"What break, if you don't mind me asking?"

When she didn't immediately answer, I thought for sure I was hitting a brick wall. I continued. "I didn't mean to be so blunt. It's just not usual to see a single woman come up here."

I could tell my face colored.

"I mean, there are single women here, but not many come up by themselves."

She bit the inside of her cheek, then said, "Well, I'm not really single. My husband's on one of his business trips, and I'm tired of sitting at home. So, I decided to break out and do something for myself for a change."

I gave a slight nod. "I admire that."

I was studying her when she asked, "What about you? What do you do up here?"

I tilted my chair onto the two back legs to try to relax, and every time I did that, I couldn't help but think about my mother reminding me not to.

"I'm a carpenter by trade. I also build homes now and then. So I stay pretty busy."

"Have you lived up here your entire life? I wouldn't have thought there were a lot of business opportunities up here."

"Yup," I said. "I tried moving down once when I was seeing someone, but it didn't work out very well for me. I wanted to be up here and she wanted to be down there. And my work was up here."

I shrugged my shoulders, which I often did when I couldn't think of anything else to add.

"Even if I was over the moon in love, I knew I'd never really be happy if I moved away."

I wasn't sure why I even added that.

"I'm sorry," Annie said.

Her lunch came, so I said, "Well, I've interrupted your lunch, so I'll let you go."

I stood, then said, "If you find you need something to do at night, there's a local cowboy bar just across the street. It's very casual, and you don't need to wear boots."

I could see the beginning of a smile form, and I smiled back.

"Thanks. I'll keep that in mind. I'm sure I'll be looking for things to do."

Then I looked down at her heeled shoes and said, "I *do* suggest that if you're going to be here for a while, you get out of those *city* shoes and put on tennis shoes. Or mountain boots."

"I'll keep that in mind, too."

I took a chance and gave her a big grin. And when she smiled back, I knew at least I hadn't completely struck out. That just made it harder for me to not think about her all night.

Most mornings I stopped at Ginny's in town before I headed for work—I'd found a good breakfast kept me going without a break until early afternoon. I wore my hair long and after my shower, I pulled it back into a short ponytail. I felt like a new man in a clean shirt and clean work jeans. When I got to Ginny's, an older man was trying to open the door and I could tell he was struggling a little bit, so I held it open for him and his wife. Over the years, I'd seen a number of older people in town, and I was always curious if they came up here when they were younger and now they were too old to move back down. Seeing this couple now, I couldn't help but wonder how they got along when it snowed...

The smells of breakfast quickly reminded me why I was there, and then I looked for a place to sit. It was surprisingly busy for a weekday, but I headed to the back of the restaurant, where I could usually find a place to sit.

I stopped dead in my tracks—I would have recognized her anywhere. There in a booth sat Annie, looking at one of the home magazines from the racks outside the door. As soon as I approached her table, she held up her empty glass of iced tea, no doubt thinking I was one of the waitresses. It caught her by surprise when she saw it was me, and I swore I saw a patch of pink color her cheeks.

"You need to quit following me," I said. She looked pretty as a picture sitting there in a black sweater. I couldn't help myself, and I grinned like a Cheshire cat, thinking I'd caught her again.

"*Me* following *you*?" she said, putting her hand to her chest. "*You're* following *me*," and she broke into an open and friendly smile.

"Mind if I join you?" I asked as I slid into the booth across from her. I'd pushed the envelope by assuming she'd be okay with it.

"I guess you already did," she said, raising those eyebrows again.

"Hey, Molly," I called to the waitress. "I'll have the Hungry Man breakfast and a strong cup of coffee."

"What else is new?" Molly said, cracking a wry smile.

"I guess you're a regular here?" Annie asked.

"Yup. If you live up here long enough, you're bound to become a regular just about everywhere you go."

"I have that at home, at some of the restaurants I go to a lot."

Why would a woman like her go to restaurants by herself, I wondered, and before I could ask, she said, "My husband is always working and my schedule is all over the place, so I end up eating on my own a lot."

I wanted to know what kind of husband let this beautiful creature wander about by herself, so I asked, "What does your husband do?"

"He's an attorney. He refers to himself as a 'slip and fall' guy."

I was sure I wrinkled my forehead in thought, for she answered my next question without me even asking it.

"He's kind of a jerk, but if you need something done, he's the one to do it."

Annie's breakfast came, and I watched her eat.

"How long have you been married?" I asked.

"Almost nine years," she said, watching my expression turn to surprise. "I was a child bride," she said with a smile.

"Wow," was all I could think of to say. "Do you have kids?"

I knew I was asking for the full lowdown on her, but I figured I might as well ask as long as she was willing to share. She didn't seem to mind my questions..

"No. Kids weren't on the menu. But I knew that when I signed up. He came with a family. And you?"

"Nah," I said. I'd already told her about my one failed romance, so I figured I might as well tell her about the other one. "It's another sob story," I said. "We never officially got engaged, but we talked about marriage. Eventually she said she wasn't ready to settle down, and looking back on it, neither was I. However, she wasted no time marrying someone else not long after we split up."

Molly set my breakfast down, and I spread butter on my pancakes.

"So I guess that's two for two," I said. "I wasn't meant to be with either lady."

"It doesn't look like you're very lucky in love," Annie said.

Did she look amused?

HOW TO LEAVE A REVIEW

If you enjoy my books, please take a moment to leave a review. It's a wonderful way to let other readers learn about new authors and books.

Amazon.com
1. Go to the product detail page for the book
2. Select Review this Product
3. Write a product review in the Customer Reviews section
4. Select a Star Rating (4 or 5 stars)
5. A Green check mark shows you've successfully submitted ratings
6. Follow my profile to keep up to date with my new books

BookBub.com
1. Click on the book to go to its BookBub page
2. From this page, select Review to give the book a star rating or to leave a review
3. Afterward, if you'd like to share your review, visit the book's page on BookBub and scroll down until you see your review.
4. Follow my profile to keep up to date with my new books

Goodreads.com
1. Click on the book to go to its Goodreads page
2. Write your review in the Give Feedback form
3. Leave a Star Rating (4 or 5 stars)
4. Check the "Post Review to Goodreads"
5. Submit your review
6. Follow my profile to keep up to date with my new books

THE MAN IN CABIN NUMBER FIVE, BOOK ONE

When Annie Parker discovers her husband's infidelity, she doesn't let it destroy her. She packs her bags and heads to Lake Arrowhead, California, the mountainside town where her family used to summer. Immersing herself in the restoration of seven 1920s-era cabins, Annie begins to put the pieces of her life back together. But starting over is never easy.

Alyce Murphy needs closure. When she discovers her father did not die from a heart attack, as she's been led to believe for the last 30 years, but in a murder/suicide, she is determined to uncover the truth of his death. But when she visits the cabin where her father ended his life, Alyce has to accept she may never know the true story.

Annie is looking toward her future while Alyce needs to put the past to rest. In parallel stories, both women are drawn to the rustic mountainside cabins as they search for the missing pieces—but they soon discover that the cabins have their own stories to tell.

THE GIRLS IN CABIN NUMBER THREE, BOOK TWO

In book two of the Guest Book Trilogy, eighty-one-year-old Annie Parker recounts taking on, against the wishes of her new love Noah, an out-of-town design project that leads her down a path that is more than she bargained for.

Back in Lake Arrowhead, California, a long-awaited mystery is buried in Cabin Number Three. Annie meets Carrie Davis who wants to update her childhood home on the lake and feels a tie to Annie's cabins. Apparently, Carrie's parents stayed here during the Roaring '20s when Bugsy Siegel ran an underground speakeasy and distillery. Unconvinced, Annie decides to investigate and finds their names in the old guest books—Elizabeth Davis and Thomas Meyer. As exciting as that sounds, it's only the start of a winding tale that Carrie and the new man in her life uncover. The pair unravel a family history filled with gangsters, working girls, and a surprising twist to a family tree.

The Girls in Cabin Number Three combines women's fiction with romance, cozy noir mystery, and suspense—all wrapped up in the majestic environs of this lovely lakeside haven.

THE STARLET IN CABIN NUMBER SEVEN, BOOK THREE

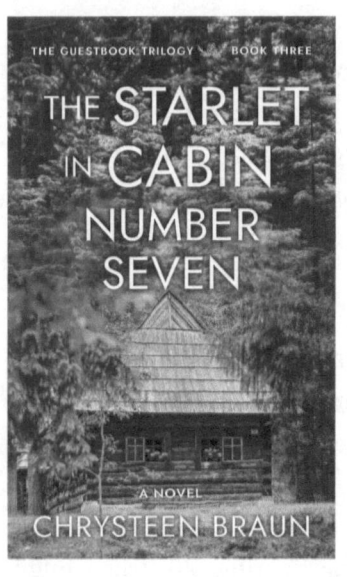

Return to picturesque 1980s Lake Arrowhead, California where another cozy cabin sheltered amongst the sweeping pine-lined vistas holds a long-buried secret, waiting to be divulged.

In this third installment of The Guest Book Trilogy, a young Annie Parker is struggling to overcome her grief over the recent loss of her sister, when a childhood friend unexpectedly turns up seeking refuge from an ill-fated marriage. It would have been easy for Annie to sink deeper into sadness, but when she learns her newest design client, Hudson Fisher, is the son of the late film actress Celeste Williams, her curiosity is peaked. As it turns out, the Roaring 20s starlet was no stranger to the Lake Arrowhead cabins—and this revelation sparks the unraveling of a scandalous story from Hollywood's bygone era. Did an illicit romance between this leading lady and her dashing costar take place in Cabin No. 7? What really went on behind-the-scenes during the filming of that silent picture? Will discovering a piece of the past bring closure to Annie's present?

A heartwarming tale of friendships, forgiveness, and a touch of old Hollywood glamour, *The Starlet in Cabin Number Seven* will have readers captivated from beginning to end.

DEAR NOAH:
THE CONCLUSION,
BOOK FIVE

Now in her mid-eighties, Annie Parker reflects on a life shaped both by heartbreak and healing. Her journey began with a life-altering decision to start anew, dedicating herself to restoring a collection of 1920s-era cabins, each rich with its own story. Through this labor of love, she wove together the memoires of her past with the promise of her future.

In *Dear Noah*, Annie reflects on her passionate love affair with Noah Chambers, a relationship filled with joy and laughter but overshadowed by an ominous prophecy from an Indian fortune teller. As their love story unfolds, the prophecy casts a long shadow, leaving Annie alone and mourning.

Seeking refuge from her sorrow, Annie moves to Prescott, California, hoping for a new beginning near her mother. There, she meets Phillip, the charming owner of the local antique shop, who help her navigate the complexities of love, loss, and second chances. Through the stories embedded in the cabins and her evolving relationships, Annie discovers that life still holds surprises, and that healing is possible at any stage.

Dear Noah: The Conclusion is a tale of love, loss, and the rediscovery of hope in life's later years. It offers a poignant exploration of resilience and the enduring strength of the human spirit, reminding readers that it's never too late to embrace hope and love.

WHEN THE DAFFODILS BLOOM: CHARLOTTE'S STORY, BOOK SIX

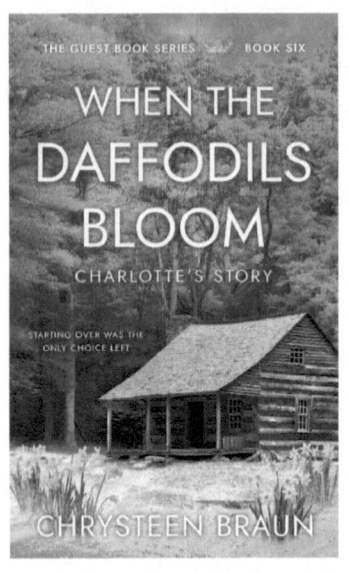

Another story of love, friendships, and new beginnings with a touch of mystery for fans of The Guest Book Series. All books can be read as stand-alones.

In the 1920s, Charlotte Hayes grew up in a small, dusty Texas town where she and her mother dreamed of one day opening a diner; a place filled with warmth, laughter, and home-cooked meals. When her mother dies, Charlotte carries that dream with her to California, determined to find a new beginning.

A housekeeper in a luxurious hotel by day, at night she sings in the smoky lounge to make ends meet. She falls in love but is pulled into a web of mobsters, and when she witnesses a killing in one of the hotel suites, she knows staying in Los Angeles isn't an option.

She flees to the quiet refuge of the Lake Arrowhead Mountains, to her friend Ruth Landry, *(The Maidservant in Cabin Number One)* and while rebuilding her life, she takes a detour when she reluctantly marries a man with ties to the Tudor House and Bugsy Siegel. After his death, she's alone again, but discovers he's left her with a shoebox filled with his memories and money.

With grit and determination, she restores a fire-damaged building in town and opens her diner. The only thing she's missing now is love. Her heart still waits for it to find her.